P9-DVQ-344

HAPPILY EVER AFTER

Sleepers Awake

Sleepers
Awake

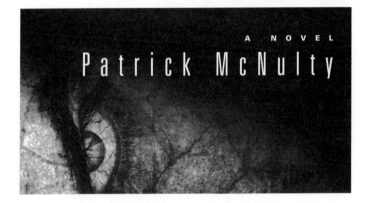

A NOVEL

Patrick McNulty

KÜNATI

CLEARWATER | FL | USA

SLEEPERS AWAKE
Copyright © 2009 by Patrick McNulty

All Rights Reserved. Published and printed in the United States of America by Kunati Inc. (USA)
and simultaneously printed and published in Canada by Kunati Inc. (Canada)
No part of this book may be reproduced, copied or used in any form
or manner whatsoever without written permission,
except in the case of brief quotations in reviews and critical articles.

For information, contact Kunati Inc., Book Publishers in Canada.
USA: 13575 58th Street North, Suite 200, Clearwater, FL 33760-3721 USA
Canada: 75 First Street, Suite 128, Orangeville, ON L9W 5B6 CANADA.
E-mail: info@kunati.com.

FIRST EDITION

Designed by Kam Wai Yu
Persona Corp. | www.personaco.com

ISBN 978-1-60164-166-3   EAN 9781601641663
Fiction

Published by Kunati Inc. (USA) and Kunati Inc. (Canada).
Provocative. Bold. Controversial.™

http://www.kunati.com

TM—Kunati and Kunati Trailer are trademarks owned by Kunati Inc.
Persona is a trademark owned by Persona Corp.
All other trademarks are the property of their respective owners.

Disclaimer: This is a work of fiction. All events described herein are imaginary, including settings and characters. Any similarity to real persons, entities, or companies is purely coincidental and not intended to represent real places or living persons. Real brand names, company names, names of public personalities or real people may be employed for credibility because they are part of our culture and everyday lives. Regardless of context, their use is meant neither as endorsement nor criticism: such names are used fictiously without intent to describe their actual conduct or value. All other names, products or brands are inventions of the author's imagination. Kunati Inc. and its directors, employees, distributors, retailers, wholesalers and assigns disclaims any liability or responsibility for the author's statements, words, ideas, criticisms or observations. Kunati assumes no responsibility for errors, inaccuracies, or omissions.

Library of Congress Cataloging-in-Publication Data

McNulty, Patrick (Patrick Karl)
Sleepers awake : a novel / Patrick McNulty. -- 1st ed.
    p. cm.
Summary: "A sleepy small town in Alaska becomes the battleground for an ancient race bent on destroying humankind and the supernatural bounty hunter dispatched to stop them"--Provided by publisher.
ISBN 978-1-60164-166-3
I. Title.
PR9199.4.M4565S64 2009
813'.6--dc22

                    2009005120

To Jenn, my wife,

for always believing in me

BEFORE THE DARK

November 13, 1976

With only minutes to live, he crawled, covered in blood, up his basement steps. Moaning and grunting with the effort, he pulled himself over the threshold into the kitchen, closed the door behind him, and secured the metal bolt. He would have prayed for the bolt to hold, but he was too tired.

At thirty-six, he was a young man, healthy, full of vigor, handsome, but sprawled across the kitchen floor, he looked like a man twice his age. His loose, wrinkled skin was the color of ash. His face was smeared with soot and blood that plastered his short black hair tight to his skull. His normally clear blue eyes were glazed, jacked wide with fear. They darted in every direction, scanning everything and nothing.

He dragged himself across the green linoleum, leaving a wide smear of blood as his bony hands clawed for purchase, fighting for every inch. When he reached the oven, he opened the door and turned the gas to HIGH. With that done he had little left to do but sit and wait and apply what pressure he could to the vertical gash that ran from his abdomen to his sternum.

A river of warm blood flowed through his thin fingers as he sat listening for the footsteps that would eventually come. For now all he heard was the hiss of gas and the crackle of the fire eating its way through the basement ceiling.

Maybe she was dead, he thought. Maybe …

His breathing grew shallower, his heart slowed, coming

down off the adrenaline boost that had got him up off that basement floor and all the way to the kitchen. His sight grew dim, curling in at the edges. Soon he would sleep.

A coil of barbed wire shivered in his belly, ripping him back to this world when the first footstep dropped heavily onto the riser in the basement. His heart trip-hammered, slamming painfully against the cage of his ribs. His body shook violently.

The footsteps grew closer as they charged up the stairs. The wounded man imagined its legs moving like pistons as it picked up speed with every step. He braced himself.

The impact nearly ripped the door off its hinges. The solitary bolt bent in its cradle. The door showered splinters of wood and plaster dust, but it held.

The other side of the door was where chaos lived.

The frenzied thing flew into a rage, fuelled by frustration and survival, clawing at the door, digging its nails into the wood, slamming its body against the frame again and again as tendrils of black smoke curled into the kitchen through the gaps between the basement door and its frame.

He couldn't move even if he had wanted to. And he wanted to, desperately. The door creaked and groaned as the bombardment wore down its defenses. He felt the heat of the flames climbing the stairs. He choked and coughed as he swallowed smoke. His vision swam from breathing the gas. He wondered how long the door would last. Would it be long enough?

The door shuddered violently with one last blow, and a two-foot crack ripped up the center. A pale arm snaked through the gap, its little fingers searching wildly for the locking bolt. The man whispered. It wasn't a prayer exactly, more of a plea. He begged forgiveness, for what exactly he wasn't sure. But there was nothing left to do. He hoped God would understand.

The pale hand found the bent bolt and slipped it out of its cradle. The door swung wide. Darkness and light flooded in together. The figure was clothed in flame as it charged across the kitchen floor, arms outstretched, reaching, searching, screaming.

The man whispered, "I'm sorry."

In the next breath, a hurricane of flame obliterated the house.

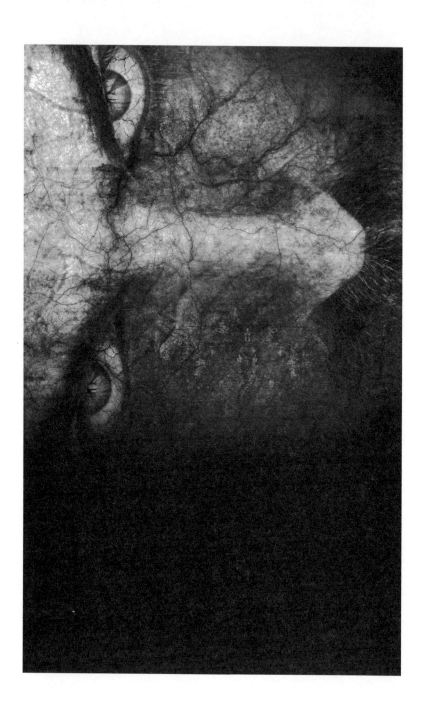

CHAPTER 1

Thick white snowflakes fell in lazy spirals out of the darkness and passed straight through the wraith in the black suit and fedora. Oliver Dannon moved with purpose across the dimly lit street and slipped silently into the passenger seat of a Cadillac CTS. Almost instantly the temperature inside the vehicle dropped like a stone. The wraith's image trembled like a desert mirage as he settled in the plush leather seat.

Behind the wheel sat Bishop Kane. Black hair cut short atop a bone-white face, strong chin and eyes so black they seemed to absorb the light around them. To Oliver, he looked very much the image of death. The Grim Reaper. And he was.

Bishop's long pale fingers drummed restlessly on the steering wheel.

"How many?" Bishop asked.

"Three," Oliver replied. "All asleep on the second floor."

Bishop slipped from the vehicle and made his way up the street through the shadows. It was just past two in the morning and Malberry Street was quiet. The snow quickly covered everything in a thick white shroud. At the back door he teased his way through the lock with a thin metal tool, then slipped as silently as smoke into the home of James Rayford and his family.

Tomorrow, when asked if they knew the Rayfords, the neighbors, friends and coworkers of the family would say of course they knew them. They played golf together almost every Saturday, they were on the same PTA. They would say that they were decent people, polite neighbors, good workers, and that Jeremy, their nine-year-old son, was an excellent student and a well-behaved young man. He was on the lacrosse team at his school. They weren't perfect, but who was? They were your average American family. Friendly, harmless, invisible.

Inside the house there was nothing unusual or ostentatious, merely the normal trappings of middle-class life—a lazy-boy recliner, X-Box, big-screen TV—but Bishop paused in the living room. Above the fireplace hung a painting, a beautiful and eerie depiction of a ship at sea. Now Bishop wasn't much for art, but he did know the difference between dogs playing poker and true talent. Even in the weak light that spilled in from the streetlamps, Bishop could tell the artist was a master. The dark and stormy sea, the vessel turning on its side, these images were very well executed, but there was something else, something within the painting, something ... hidden. Bishop took a step closer to the canvas and stopped. For a moment he thought the image trembled. He realized that he had been holding his breath. He took a step back and turned away without a backward glance.

Bishop climbed the carpeted steps to the second floor. He passed pictures of the loving family at birthday parties, ski trips, around Christmas trees opening presents. In all the pictures, they smiled and grinned for the camera. A family very much in love, he thought. At the second floor he crossed the hall to the third door on the left.

He killed young Jeremy first.

CHAPTER 2

Bishop Kane sat silently in a chair opposite the very cold and very sore James Rayford, savoring the moment. It had taken Bishop seven months, traveling through three different countries, to finally catch up with the man seated before him. He wasn't going to let this end quickly.

Rayford writhed uncomfortably on the metal chair. His arms were stretched painfully behind him, his hands shackled together through the bars of the metal chair he sat on. A cloth bag covered his head. He shook his head in the hopes of dislodging it, but it was tied just under his chin.

His hooded head swung left and right, searching for something, anything that would give him a point of bearing.

"Hello?" he croaked. A wracking cough bent him at the waist. His body shuddered. When the coughing subsided he shifted in his seat and realized that his ankles were also chained to the legs of the chair.

"Hello?" he begged. "Answer me, please!"

Bishop's footsteps rang out like shotgun blasts over the bare concrete.

"Hello? Hello?" James pleaded. "Please."

Bishop untied the drawstring on the bag that covered Rayford's head and tossed it aside. On paper, James Rayford was forty-two, but tonight he looked a lot older. Naked and pale, he was small and shriveled. Bishop could see that, in his day, he had once been athletic, maybe a long distance runner. He had that kind of frame. Tall, skinny. Knobby knees and shoulders. Definitely no contact sports for little Jimmy. But as James entered middle age, his runner's body was running to fat. A pale little paunch sat in his lap like a hairless cat, and what was left of his brown hair was losing the battle to gray. He looked like an eighth-grade science teacher, the one everyone hoped they wouldn't get. The only color on his body was the dark purple bruise that threatened to swell his right eye shut.

Bishop couldn't help but smile, reliving that memory, watching Rayford's eyes roll open sleepily, slowly, his brain a little behind the game, trying to process what the eyes were seeing. Then the combination of shock and horror as Bishop loomed above him. In his house. In his bedroom. Then BAM! Bishop drove a right fist into the side of his head and fired the tranquilizer gun into his throat. Perfection.

"What is this?" Rayford asked. "Who are you? Where am I? Where's Jeremy? Where's Linda?"

"So many questions."

"Please."

"Please what?"

"Tell me where Jeremy is?"

"He's at home. In his bed. Dead."

Rayford's face seemed to crack and collapse in on itself. His eyes were swollen with tears that ran down his cheeks. He made a low moan in his throat. Bishop recognized the anguished sound when he heard it. He had made it once before himself. So far he was impressed with Mr. Rayford. He was good.

"And my wife?"

"Do I have to say the words?" Bishop replied. "I'm afraid

they didn't make the cut, as it were. They just weren't as important as you, Jimmy."

Rayford lunged toward Bishop but the metal chair was bolted to the ground and the chains held. He strained and snapped. Spittle and snot and tears ran down his face.

"I'll kill you! You motherfucker! You hear me? I will cut your fucking head off!"

Rayford strained and flexed and pulled, but all he managed to do was cut his wrists deeper with the cuffs. Blood flowed through his fingers, dripping steadily onto the concrete floor.

When the fight left him he whispered, "I'll kill you." Surprisingly, he thrashed again. He pulled on his cuffs hard enough for Bishop to believe that he might pop off a hand and come at him with his bloody stump. But the hand held, and soon, defeated, James Rayford slumped in his chair and wept, sniffling and dripping into his lap.

Bishop took a long look at Rayford and smiled a small thin smile with all the mirth of a Great White.

"That was very good," he said.

James Rayford looked up stupidly.

"I mean, if I didn't know you—"

"You don't know me," Rayford spat.

"And I didn't know what you are, I would have thought that you actually cared for those things back there."

Rayford looked up. "They were my family."

Bishop leaned close enough to smell the sweat and snot and tears rising off Mr. Rayford.

"Fuck your family. They're dead. Stone-cold fucking tag-on-a-toe dead, but here's the good news: you won't be too far behind them." Bishop shot out a right hand that snapped

Rayford's head back on his neck and shattered his nose. Blood exploded across his face and chest.

"Who is Eve?" Bishop asked.

CHAPTER 3

December 10, 2007

The woods were deep and quiet and still. Snow sifted silently down from a twilit sky painted by a dying sun in brilliant reds, oranges and gold. The fields seemed to burn as the shadows lengthened like wild vines in the growing darkness. In Danaid, Alaska it was just past one in the afternoon, but in this part of the world, at this time of year, sunlight was a precious commodity. Locals called this time of year the Dark Season.

He had to admit the old man was fast.

Randy Tinsel dipped his right shoulder and angled his snowmobile through the line of snow-covered evergreens, deftly navigating the drifting terrain as Rage Against the Machine screamed in his ears.

Since he and his father had left Route 4, he figured that this time, finally, he had him. His dad had cut wide right to follow the river, while Randy opted for the more direct, albeit dangerous route through the forest. He gunned the throttle, felt the machine respond and jerk forward and cut across the fresh powder, swerving around trees, cresting peaks and dropping down into valleys of the terrain that had been his second home for the last twenty-seven years.

A smile broke as Randy relished the thought of finally beating the old man to the mine. No mean feat, but it was inevitable, he thought. Only a matter of time until the young warrior overtook the old, the student became the teacher. It was the way of the world. Survival of the fittest.

Every year their annual hunting trip began the same way, with the race to the mine. Randy's mother didn't like to hear them talk about it because it involved riding machines with little or no protection other than a helmet and snow gear while traveling at high speeds over unpredictable terrain. Moms are like that. So they didn't talk about it. They didn't have to. It was understood.

Randy switched on his headlight as twilight finally bled away to night. Deepening shadows blurred the edges and filled in the gaps of the landscape as the last trace of amber light was smothered into extinction. He wasn't frightened by the dark or the reduced visibility. He was well familiar with this area and this path in particular. It would take more than nightfall for him to let up on the throttle, much less turn back.

Randy guided the sled down a sharp decline and dropped into a narrow channel of closely cropped evergreens. Their sharp needles slapped and scratched at his helmet as he powered through the gauntlet, but it didn't matter. He was close.

As Randy negotiated the last stand of trees before the clearing, he almost felt sorry for the old man. Tragic, really, but inevitable. In another second he exploded into a clearing enveloped in a cloud of fresh powder. His powerful halogen headlight swept over the crumbling remains of the mining office. Broken windows, bare cinderblock scrawled with graffiti, and from beneath a blue plastic tarp a piece of reflector tape winked at him mockingly.

Son of a bitch.

Randy powered the sled toward the flickering bar of light

and found his father's snowmobile neatly stored beneath a quickly made lean-to constructed from a rusted piece of corrugated steel.

Unbelievable. Not only had his father beat him here, but he had enough time to secure the tarp to the machine and set up the lean-to.

Randy was still shaking his head as he baby-stepped his sled in alongside his father's and adjusted the tarp to cover both sleds. He replaced his helmet with a knitted watch cap, pulled off his gloves and pressed STOP on his MP3 player, silencing Rage Against the Machine halfway through "Bulls on Parade." The silence rushed him from all sides like a pack of wild dogs. There was no wind. Thick snowflakes steadily tumbled, burying the world in white. His breathing, ragged and wheezy, was loud and clear in his ears. It was not the first time lately that he found himself out of breath during relatively easy tasks. He promised himself, again, that he would quit smoking. After the holidays.

Out here in God's country, miles from the constant whine of tires on asphalt, away from the hum of power lines, ringing phones, screeching computer modems searching for a connection, and screaming neighbors, every sound was magnified. The snow packed down and crunched under his feet, his nylon suit swished as he stepped out from under the metal awning. He stared up at the cold light of the brilliant stars that now crowded the sky, and he remembered how much he had missed them. The last six months, Randy had been in California, attending UCLA, finishing up his degree in biotechnology. He loved California, but in most areas, stars were little more than myth.

Randy ripped open a Velcro pocket. He withdrew a small but powerful Maglite flashlight and swept its beam over the front entrance to the mine.

Where was Dad?

It wasn't like him to not be waiting when he arrived. To gloat, sure, but also to make sure that Randy made it to the mine in one piece. His father loved competition and he loved to win, but it all took a backseat to safety.

From another, larger pocket Randy extracted a walkie-talkie that his mother had purchased the day before at the Trading Post in town and had insisted they carry. Randy squeezed the TALK button.

"How the hell did you get here so fast?"

His breath smoked in the frosty air. He let go of the button and listened to the low hiss of static, waiting for the reply. He stood there a good two minutes, getting colder by the second, waiting. He shuffled from foot to foot, sweeping his light over the awning, the two sleds, the gap in the evergreens where he had entered the clearing. All was still save the falling snow.

Again he pressed the TALK button. "Dad?"

The dead air sounded ominous, like a low chant whispered just beneath the surface of his understanding, a message hidden in the white noise. Had his father turned on his walkie-talkie, or brought it along at all for that matter? Neither scenario would surprise him. His father was old school to the nth degree. He came out to the wilderness to be one with nature, to live off the land and experience a connection between man and nature that couldn't be found in the cities. He carried nothing that he wouldn't use. No fancy gadgets, no battery-powered socks. Thinking back, Randy remembered his father's face when his mother presented them with the walkie-talkies. The way he eyed the digital screen, and the myriad of tiny buttons and knobs with the kind of naked revulsion one would normally employ when gazing upon a bizarre new breed of insect.

Randy tried one last time and then pocketed the radio, leaving it on, just in case. He and his father had been coming out to the mine to camp and hunt since before Randy could even hold a rifle. He knew his father's favorite haunts. He wasn't worried. If he knew his dad, he was up there on the second floor right now setting up camp. Always one to look on the bright side, Randy pinched a cigarette from a crumpled pack and sparked the end. He knew his father hated his smoking and considered smoking in the clean cold mountain air the highest form of sacrilege. So, this little snub out here at the entrance delivered his last chance to light up. He dragged deep on the filter, filling his lungs with the poison of nicotine and a million other carcinogens with names he couldn't begin to pronounce. And he felt better. With his Maglite leading the way, he stepped over the crumbling entranceway into the darkness of the interior.

The Monk's Head Mine had been closed for more than forty years. The front office of the once profitable venture was set right into the face of Monk's Head Mountain, named for three separate mountains that seemed to form a balding dome, bordered on either side by smaller peaks giving the range the appearance of a traditional monk's head.

In the summer it was the preferred make-out spot of all the locals, where on any given Friday night at least two or three cars would be parked inconspicuously around the crumbling structure, their windows fogged up like a greenhouse. But now, nearing the end of December, only the most desperate lovers made the trek up the winding dirt road, covered in snow and usually blocked by a felled tree. But if you were looking for a little private shelter, a place out of the way that guaranteed a winter of solitude, it was definitely your spot.

Randy's footfalls over the rotting wood floor echoed hollowly off the cinderblock walls. On his back he carried an orange backpack. Across the top of the pack rested a rifle, concealed from the elements in a black leather case.

With all the gaps in the walls and the broken windows, the building wasn't much warmer than outside, but at least he was dry and out of the falling snow. He unwrapped the scarf from his face and dusted the snow and ice from his blonde goatee. He sat his tinted goggles on top of his head and scanned the interior of the place.

He found himself in a short gray hallway without windows. Graffiti advising him to go fuck himself and that Sally B is a real slut were written in red and took up most of the wall space. Sweeping his flashlight beam, he spotted remains of previous inhabitants—an ancient campfire, a small pile of cans and clothes, bits of wood stacked against the wall.

And the small burning eyes of a wolf that glittered in the sudden light like drops of fire.

Randy froze.

The wolf did not move. Its body lay crumpled against the wall, blood spilling from its mouth to puddle around its large head. Its hind legs were horribly twisted, thin leg bones poking free from its matted fur like splinters of ivory. Randy figured that the wolf had challenged another for the same scrap of food and lost. Mortally wounded the wolf had shuffled inside the building to die. The theory held water, at least until he looked at the wall above the wolf's corpse.

The wall was smeared with blood about five feet above the floor, as if the wolf had been thrown. What could throw a wolf with enough force to kill it? Randy stroked the matted fur of the wolf's head and felt the shards of skull just beneath the skin like broken bits of pottery.

Right about then Randy got that little twinge in the belly, a little ice in his bowels. Something was not right. Not a big something, but a lot of little ones all lined up in a row like dominoes. Randy had never been very intuitive, but he was definitely picking up a bad vibe now. A moment ago the mine had been a palace filled with childhood memories, which, for the most part, he could look back on fondly. Now every shadow seemed to hold menace. He suddenly realized just how isolated they were out here. Totally alone. Anything could happen. No one would hear. No one would know. It was a twenty-minute sled ride into the deepest part of the forest. They were in a building with no road access. They weren't due back for three days. If anything went wrong they would have to wait it out until his mother missed them.

A noise like the shuffle and scrape of a footstep yanked Randy out of his paranoid ramblings. He swung the flashlight in a circle, illuminating the pathetic contents of the near-empty room, finding nothing but garbage and more shadows.

Randy unslung his backpack and removed his rifle from its leather case. After checking that it was fully loaded, he switched the safety off. Whatever killed the wolf had to be either much larger or rabid or both. Something very strong and very big. Something Randy would rather encounter holding a loaded rifle.

With his pack replaced, he carried his rifle in his right hand, cradling the stock in his elbow, and his flashlight in his left. He moved forward through the reception area to a wrought iron staircase that spiraled upward, disappearing into the shadows of the second floor. At the base of the staircase, Randy swept his flashlight, again proving that he was indeed alone. His father had always camped on the second floor in one of the executive offices, but the stairs were loose, the whole structure twisted underfoot, swaying as if he were walking up a mast pole in high winds. So he waited, resting one foot on the first riser and feeling horribly exposed. Exposed to what, he had no idea and didn't want to know.

"Dad?" he called. He waited, but only the wind moaned a reply. He began to climb.

The ancient staircase creaked and groaned under his weight as the bolts shifted in place, releasing little clouds of rust with every step. When he reached the second floor he went straight through a pair of heavy double doors into a conference room where two of the walls were glass. During the day the view would be breathtaking, but here in the dark there was only his grimy reflection shining his light over the room.

At the north end of the room was another set of double doors, their edges defined by lines of harsh white light. He stepped through the doors. His dad's small collapsible halogen lamp lit the room generously, revealing his dad's open pack. It looked as though his father had begun setting up but never finished. His pack was open and his sleeping bag unrolled, but the small camp stove was in pieces and their tent still rolled in its sack.

Randy called out once again, a little edge in his voice, a little panic. His dad was a lot of things, but disappearing acts in the wilderness was not his style. Sure, he'd hide and maybe jump out at you in the woods, but he hadn't done that since Randy was nine. Randy doubted it would be a good time to start trying that shit while he carried a high-powered rifle.

Where the hell is he?

Randy called a third time. His voice trembled, warbling a little like a scared kid of twelve, not a man of nearly thirty.

He made his way across the room to a door marked STAIRS, where his light caught a flash of color.

Yellow.

Randy ran to where his father's parka lay in a heap on the floor. Puffs of white stuffing bled from where the coat had been ripped up the back, nearly slicing it in two. He held the coat up to his face and smelled the familiar mix of sweat and his father's cologne. A snake of ice-cold fear curled and snapped in his belly. A thin sheen of sweat broke out over his body.

Randy searched the coat and found his father's flashlight, matches, a compass, a pen, a notepad. A thin metal canister contained two cigars—victory cigars, his father called them, awarded to the hunter after the kill. Cigars were not cigarettes. Cigars were civilized, and therefore did not defile the purity of the great outdoors.

The walkie-talkie was missing.

That is, if he had brought it at all.

He brought it, Randy thought. Mom would make sure he did. Randy fumbled open the Velcro pocket and retrieved his radio. He pushed the TALK button. In the stillness of the mining office, the answering click sounded like a snapping bone.

"Dad?"

It was hard to pinpoint where the sound came from, but he had a sinking feeling he knew where he should look.

Every year that he and his father had come here to hunt, he had found this same door, the one leading down into the mine, and as always he had found it locked, sealed by the local authorities to keep overly curious kids from getting lost inside one of the winding tunnels or dropping into a sinkhole never to return.

But now the doorknob sat almost parallel to the door, the steel around it puckered, as if someone had wrenched it to the left until the bolt sprang free of the lock. Someone of incredible strength. Someone who could kill a wolf by throwing it against a wall. The thought froze his hand, hovering over the twisted doorknob.

At that instant, he knew his father was dead, killed by some horrible thing that was no longer interested in wolves. Images of his father being bled, hung by his ankles, his green eyes frosted over like so many deer they had taken from this forest, crowded his thoughts until he had to close his eyes and shake his head to clear his mind.

After a moment he found he could breathe again. He took a few deep breaths just to be sure, grabbed the warped doorknob, opened the creaking metal door and slipped into the darkness.

Beyond the doorway lay a set of metal stairs that spiraled down through the heart of the mine. Standing on the first stair he once again pushed the TALK button on his radio. The answering click was louder.

He moved as soundlessly as possible, but the steel stairs

shook and clanged, announcing every step. He traded stealth for speed and moved quickly down, keeping his light trained on the next riser while his finger hovered over the trigger of his rifle.

At the first floor access door, he tried the radio and again discovered that the radio was further down in the mine. Finally he hit the rock floor.

Standing on the rough floor several stories underground gave Randy the feeling of being on another planet. His light washed over the pock-marked walls, shored up with ancient timber and iron. It was colder down here, a damp cold that soaked through his many layers to penetrate bone and pool in the pit of his stomach.

Another tap of the radio and the sound of a pistol crack made him jump and give a little yelp. Randy focused the beam down the tunnel ahead and found the radio lying in the dirt. He hit the button again and listened to the response. This time he was ready. Cautiously, he threw light over the tunnel walls and ceiling. Once he deemed that the radio was not bait for a trap, he crept over and scooped up the little gadget from the rock floor, slipping it into a front coat pocket along with its mate.

His heart picked up the pace again, smashing against his ribs. He moved slowly, his flashlight illuminating the uneven ground ahead of him twenty feet at a time. Every sound reverberated, bouncing off the rock walls. The scrape of his boots, the wheeze of his breathing, even the rustle of his clothing, all came together to create the illusion that he was not alone.

To his right, about fifteen feet away, his light found the edge of the first doorway. He followed the tunnel wall with his gloved hand until his fingers slid over the rock edge and he peered around the corner. Soft orange firelight flickered from a doorway about twenty yards down the passage.

He forced himself not to run. Anger and fear and hate boiled up inside him. As he crept down the passageway toward the orange glow, he thought that if he did indeed find his father sitting at a warm fire, sipping instant coffee, he might be tempted to shoot him. If this turned out to be some kind of rite of passage into manhood bullshit, he might even kill him. The alternative was that whoever had sliced his father's coat up the back was warming himself by the fire. The thought of killing someone, of shooting them down, of slaughtering them for harming his father made his heart beat faster. His trigger finger curled reflexively around the trigger, ready for action.

He moved to the edge of the doorway and discovered that it had been sealed until recently by a sliding metal door. The door was rusted on its rails, but someone had opened it. He pressed his face close to the wall and peered through the doorway, where the room was revealed to him an inch at a time.

The room was small, no larger than ten by ten, an old storeroom by the look of it. Empty shelving lined the walls and paper garbage rotted in the dark corners. A small dying fire burned near the center of the room, bathing his father in trembling amber light.

He lay flat on his back, his blue-gray eyes rolled up high into his head until the whites gleamed like twin moons.

It seemed to Randy that his father's skin was moving, trembling as if it were literally crawling. His father was in pain, that much was clear. Thick, ropy cords of muscle and tendon stood out on his neck as the large man's body flexed, caught in some horrible seizure. Randy gasped and took a shuffling step into the room. His father's eyes found his in the gloom and they were wide with pain and fear.

"Run, Randy!" he said through clenched teeth. "Run!"

CHAPTER 4

It had been three days since Bishop had kidnapped James Rayford. Fifteen people had died that night, but it was just a dent, one cell out of hundreds. Maybe thousands. The Ministry of the Wraith wasn't sure of their numbers, and that was the most maddening of it all, the not knowing. They desperately needed to find out who this Eve was. Was it even a woman? As far as hard facts were concerned, there weren't many, except that these insiders were getting stronger everyday.

The major cities were dangerous now, but sometimes he had no choice. His SUV was one in a long line of vehicles waiting for the light to change. Bishop scanned the sidewalks left and right. His right hand drifted to his waist, his fingers played over the pistol grip. A man carrying groceries stopped dead in his tracks to stare at him. And then another, a woman this time, pushing a small child in a stroller. They were everywhere. A young kid holding a skateboard, a man in a suit. Soldiers forever vigilant. The light turned green up ahead and the line rolled forward, but not far enough. Bishop swore and the line stopped.

His admirers hadn't moved. More and more stopped now, staring. Bishop's head snapped left and right, waiting for the attack. His pistols were out.

Tap tap tap

Bishop wheeled in his seat and found an old woman staring at him, her dirty face inches from the glass. Grime and filth had darkened her tanned skin and her once brown hair was matted and flew away from her head in ragged tangles. Her eyes were the color of jade, clear and focused.

The barrels of Bishop's guns were pointed chest level. If she so much as raised a finger to the glass he would shoot her through the door. Bishop's fingers curled over the triggers. Breathless moments passed.

She did not raise a finger. She didn't move. She simply stared for a moment, a small smile playing on her lips, and then she mouthed three words.

We see you.

The light changed and Bishop roared up the street and away, leaving the woman to watch him disappear into the distance.

The woman shuffled back to the sidewalk and the others who had been silently watching fell into step with the crowd. And just like that, they were hidden once again. Hidden in plain sight. Invisible. That was their greatest strength.

A little more than three hours north of the city, Bishop left the highway and followed poor country roads to an unmarked private drive. The twisted narrow road was crowded on either side by a dense forest. Their gnarled branches reached over the road to create a canopy of near darkness even at midday. After nearly a mile he emerged into the weak December light.

The Nazareth House was a sprawling Victorian estate that was larger than most townhouse villages. Bishop's SUV pulled into the turnaround in front of the house and parked at the foot of a wide staircase meticulously free of snow and ice. Halfway up the stairs the arched front doors opened and a tall, olive-skinned manservant greeted Bishop.

"Welcome, Mr. Kane."

With the door closed behind him the butler asked if he could take Bishop's coat. Bishop told him that he could not.

"Very well, sir. If you'll follow me."

The butler smiled politely before turning on his heel and heading up the wide staircase that spread into a landing leading right and left into the second floor.

At the top of the stairs the butler headed right and Bishop soon found himself in a long hall painted a heavy maroon, lit by a steady rail of flame that lay close to the floor. On the walls hung framed pieces of parchment. The butler moved quickly and without sound through the hall, never glancing at the framed artifacts.

They arrived at a set of tall arched doors, beautifully carved, depicting an intricate battle scene that flickered with life as it caught the weak golden light from the rail of flame below.

"Ms LeClere awaits you inside, sir."

The butler stood away from the doors, appearing quite uncomfortable to be this close to whatever lay beyond. His hands were clasped below his belt, his face set in a subservient smile.

"Do you require anything more?"

"No," Bishop replied.

"Very well, sir."

The butler smiled, nodded politely and stepped quickly back the way they had come, disappearing down the hall.

Bishop pushed through the heavy doors into the darkness within.

The library was warmly decorated in dark wood and lit by a roaring fire large enough for a Viking funeral.

Sitting in a deep leather wingback chair was the lithe frame of Madeline LeClere, her slender hand wrapped around a healthy glass of bourbon. Her pale face was coldly beautiful, with features as delicate as blown glass. Her eyes were depthless and reflected her surroundings. Staring into the fire, her eyes flashed through every color the flames had to offer, oranges, yellows and every derivation of both. As Bishop drew closer he saw that her eyes were a deep crimson.

In the weak light Bishop made out a silhouette just behind her. He was a tower of a man, six foot seven and easily three hundred and fifty pounds, which put him five inches taller and a hundred and twenty-five pounds heavier than Bishop himself. As always the man was dressed in a beautifully tailored black suit, with a crisp white shirt split down the center by a simple maroon tie. The man's bald head gleamed ghostly white, his eyes were shielded, even in this failing light, by small designer shades. Bishop had met the man several times, but knew him only as Mr. Abbadon. Besides the man's size, the only other distinguishing feature was a thin, flat scar that ran horizontally across his throat. The old wound flashed in the weak light, glinting like the knife blade that had left it.

Bishop took a seat across from Madeline in an identical wingback chair, separated from hers by a low round table. For a time, Madeline didn't face him or acknowledge that he was there. She sat and stared, concentrating on the firelight as if deciphering some hidden message within it. Bishop's impatient gaze drifted around the room from the fire to Madeline to the shadow of Mr. Abbadon who, as far as he could tell, never once took his eyes off him. Bishop gave him a little wink. Mr. Abbadon never moved. When he looked back to Madeline, she stared at him coolly.

"We have had the recording of your *interview* with James Rayford analyzed."

"And?"

The grating sound of Rayford's screams flooded the comfortable library, ripping apart the silence. He heard his own voice ask over and over again, "Where is she? Who is Eve?" There was more of Rayford screaming and then gibberish that Bishop didn't understand. Something that sounded like *tonkrit*?

"There," Madeline whispered.

The recording was rewound and the final word *tonkrit* was repeated.

"Do you hear it?" she asked.

"I hear it, but I don't know what it means."

"You asked Mr. Rayford where Eve was and he answered," she replied. "Tonk-rit is their word for home, Bishop."

Bishop threw up his hands, palms up. "Okay. So where's home?"

The corners of Madeline's mouth curled into a smile that froze the short distance between them.

"Walk with me."

Madeline led him to a room off the library. Inside the room were three paintings set up on easels for display. Each had been painted in dark, haunting shades. Each scene was vastly different, but it was obvious that the same master had created them all.

"Have you ever seen a painting like these?"

"Yes," he said. "In Rayford's house. Over his fireplace. A ship at sea. It was like these. Beautiful."

"It seems these are given to the most loyal and most trusted. Over the last seven years we have retrieved these three from homes in London, Toronto and New York. We've had our wraiths search for the artist since then. And now, together with this *home* business, it seems we have our first solid lead on Eve."

Madeline produced a small glossy paper and handed it to Bishop.

"This photo was emailed to us this morning by one of our contacts."

Bishop took the photo. Long dark hair, pale blue eyes. Beautiful.

Madeline smiled. "So like her mother."

Bishop found it hard to breathe, as if the air had been sucked out of the room. The photograph trembled in his hand.

"It's not possible," he whispered.

"She lives, Bishop," Madeline said, "and she's come home."

The face in the picture was unsmiling, but her eyes looked directly at him, as if she knew she was being photographed. She wanted to be photographed. She wanted him to come. A coldness formed in the pit of his stomach. Its icy tendrils spread quickly through his body, numbing him.

"Kill her, Bishop. Save us all."

When Bishop looked up, Madeline had left without a sound.

CHAPTER 5

She wore a paint-splattered jean shirt and panties. Her small, bare feet were freckled with paint spatter. Blushing rose red, azure blue, freshly fallen snow white.

The attic was small and heated by a droning little space heater that glowed bright orange. This was her space, from the exposed rafters to the crumbling drywall, complete with at least sixty years of peeling wallpaper and paint, accented with kids' drawings and scribbled names. It was all her own. She glided over the worn boards, relishing the smoothness of their skin, polished by her feet and the feet of a hundred others who had used the old attic for everything from a child's playroom to a local union office.

She did not use electric light in her studio. It was too harsh, too mechanical and cold for her work, for her work relied on soft, warm luminescence.

Petra painted at night, in the silence of the witching hour. When the sleepy town of Danaid was indeed asleep, she would awake. Hip deep in a flickering sea of golden candlelight, she was a creator of worlds. Her paintings were not stagnant snapshots, but a window on a strange and beautiful world that shuddered with life, a twitching, fluid present. She was a uniquely gifted artist, there was no question of that, but in the flickering candlelight the characters and scenes she created on the canvas seemed to vibrate. Backs undulated with breath, expressions darkened and bloomed with the whim of mercurial shadows. They were alive.

In her studio she was a creator. A maker of worlds. She was energy.

As she stood at the canvas, her brush poised, her entire body grew still. Her toned legs beneath the hem of the jean shirt, her delicate arms and hands, were bronzed by the warm light. Petra's blue-gray eyes scanned the scene she had created, studying every inch, every drop and smear of paint. She waited, deliberating, deciding. Her world waited for her. Finally her mouth pulled into a smile that grew, revealing a row of perfect teeth.

She was finished.

She pulled her brush from the canvas and spun on her heel. She moved with an easy grace that came only in the attic, and only in the near dark as if she were most comfortable in the shadows.

At a scarred wooden table weighted down with cans of paint and drying brushes, she dropped her brush into a hazy glass of Varsol and set her palette down carefully. She removed the top tray from a red metal toolbox and dug through its depths, knocking aside tiny jars of half-used paint and spare brushes until her hand emerged with a crumpled pack of cigarettes.

The three that remained were more than likely stale and definitely bent, but it wasn't the taste she was after. This was ritual. She struck a wooden match against the table and sparked a tiny head of flame. She inhaled deeply, savoring every atom until finally she exhaled, blowing a column of gray smoke up into the rafters.

Petra tiptoed into the bedroom with a cup of steaming coffee and winced when she saw the light of day sneaking through the cracks in the Venetian blinds. She set the coffee down gently on the bedside table and eased onto the mattress, silently scaling the bump under the covers until she straddled the mid point.

Petra held her breath as she gently pulled down the blanket until she could see his face. Still asleep, lost in dreams, his eyes were closed, his mouth slightly open, and she loved him all over again. His brown hair was flattened to his skull on one side from the pillow and his broad chest rose and fell rhythmically with his soft breath. She leaned in slowly until she could smell his stale morning breath and wrinkled her nose. Sean's eyes snapped open. Her breath caught in her throat, and before she could react she was thrown up into the air. She squealed as Sean rolled over on top of her and pinned her to the mattress. She was still laughing as he kissed her twice on the mouth.

"What are you doing in here, huh? It's only . . ." Sean said as he craned his neck to read the digital clock without letting her go, "six-thirty in the morning!"

"It's time to get up!" she said, bucking under him until they were on their sides facing each other. Petra whipped back the comforter, blasting Sean's naked body with a shot of cold air.

"Jesus! What are you doing? I'm naked under here."

"I know."

Petra slipped beneath the covers, wrapping her long legs around him, straddling him.

"Okay, this is better," Sean said, sliding his hands up over her warm thighs.

She leaned down over him and kissed him lightly on the mouth. As always she tasted vaguely of cinnamon, but today he tasted something else.

"Were you smoking?"

"Maybe," she replied.

Sean cocked an eyebrow and slid up into a sitting position, pulling away from her as she bent to kiss his chest.

"I thought you quit."

"I have, except—" she whispered, kissing the base of his throat.

"You finished it?"

Petra nodded, grinning broadly. "This morning."

"Congratulations, that's great."

Petra stopped kissing him.

"That's not enough," she said.

"It isn't?"

Petra's right hand crept down his chest, over his stomach.

"Not nearly enough."

Sean smiled. He slipped his hands down her back and pulled her a little closer.

"Well, you should be properly compensated," he said.

Petra's hand slipped easily between his legs and Sean's eyes slid closed.

"I should get something for all my hard work, don't you think?"

"Definitely," he whispered breathlessly.

Sean's hands slid up over her bare stomach, under her jean shirt.

"It's only fair," he mumbled into her neck.

Her skin was warm and soft and smelled of peaches. As he pulled her closer, she guided him inside.

Her tongue slid into his mouth, slipping over his lips. Their kiss was broken for a second as her shirt was pulled over her head. Hungrily, their mouths locked together, warm skin moving together. His mouth found her nipple and she moaned, gripping him closer.

As he pushed inside her they shared a breathless moment, but they quickly found their rhythm and were soon rocking gently.

Her fingers laced behind his head as his tongue explored her throat. For the moment everything was forgotten as they rocked faster, building toward a climax.

"Dad?"

As they always did when this happened, they pretended that they could ignore Sean's son, pretend he wasn't there, or that they didn't hear him. They gripped each other tight, trying to ward off the inevitable.

"Dad? Where are my boots?" Kevin asked from just outside the door.

"Hold on a second, Kev," Sean replied.

"Dad, I'm going to be late!"

"I'm coming! I'm coming!"

"Not before me," Petra whispered.

Petra's laugh always made Sean smile, especially this laugh, her deep-throated laugh that seemed to explode from deep within her, the one that Sean knew she couldn't control, and that she hated because of the snorting sound that usually accompanied it.

She rolled off him, trying not to giggle. Naked, she circled the bed and grabbed Sean's jean shirt and a pair of sweat pants. She buttoned the shirt quickly and wrongly. Before she left she climbed across the bed to where Sean sat against the headboard.

"You get to come and what do I get?" he said with a smile.

She winked and kissed him delicately on the mouth.

"I'll make it up to you," she whispered.

"For now I'll take the coffee," he said, reaching for the steaming mug on the bedside table.

Petra scrambled across the sheets and when Sean reached for it he found nothing but air. Petra sipped the hazelnut coffee as she stepped backward toward the bedroom door.

"Please," she said with a sly smile. "You weren't that good."

Sean flopped back down into the bed, pulling the covers over his head as she slipped out the door and into the hall.

In the hall, eight-year-old Kevin Berlin stood ready to go to hockey practice, dressed in his equipment and his heavy winter coat, but missing his boots. He looked quite distressed with his little white stocking feet sticking out from the end of his thick shin pads. He was a handsome boy, inheriting his father's easy smile.

"Hey, honey," Petra said, giving him a quick peck on the cheek. "All ready to go?"

"I can't find my—" he stopped cold when he smelled the smoke that still clung to her. "You finished your painting?"

Kevin moved slowly, almost reverently over the creaking floorboards of the attic toward the canvas. Petra was close behind, watching him intently as he neared the easel. When he got a little too close for Petra's liking, her hand slid over his shoulder, gently keeping him from touching the still wet scene.

"What do you think?" she asked.

The scene was dark and malevolent, as if seen through the gauze of fog. Forms could be made out if one stared, but as soon as they swam into focus the flickering light of the candles blurred their edges and cast the elusive characters into darkness. Kevin was mesmerized.

"Cool," he whispered. Petra beamed like a proud parent as she stood admiring her own work.

"So you like it?"

"Yeah. Oh, yeah, way better than the ones you did with the birds and stuff."

Petra stepped around Kevin, inching closer to the painting, close enough to gently trace the outline of the work's focus, the small figure of a man, without actually touching the canvas. Kevin was entranced. He reached toward the scene. His tiny fingers outstretched, desperately close to the paint.

Petra's arm shot out and roughly pushed him back a little too hard. Kevin stumbled and fell.

"Don't touch that! Ever! Do you hear me?" Petra shouted. "Do you understand?"

Kevin stared up at her. Her eyes glowed like hot coals pinning him to the floor as tears rolled over his face.

Petra spun around and bent over the painting, scrutinizing the spot where Kevin's fingers might have touched.

"It has to dry," she whispered.

When she finally determined that there was no damage, she turned from the painting with her temperature heading toward normal and found herself alone.

At the bottom of the stairs, Petra found Kevin wearing one boot and digging through a pile of possible matches in the hall closet. She whispered his name but he didn't look up or stop what he was doing. She crouched beside him, close enough to see his face in the shadow of the closet, his pale little hands sifting through piles of sandals, shoes and boots that littered the floor.

"Kevin, I'm sorry."

"Okay," he replied like it was nothing. Like an adult would, she thought, and she felt a pain in her chest.

"No, honey, I really am. Stop for a second." Petra slipped a hand over his shoulder but he pulled away, rolling into a sitting position on the opposite side of the doorway atop a pile of sneakers.

"C'mon honey, really. I'm sorry."

"You pushed me," he said, staring into his lap, his chin on his chest.

"I know, and I'm sorry. I was stupid, honey. It's . . . just a painting. I would never hurt you. You know that, don't you?"

Kevin nodded, trying not to cry.

Petra inched closer across the doorway.

"C'mon, what do you say? Friends?"

This time when she slid her palm over his cheek he didn't pull away. He leaned forward, walking on his knees into her arms. He buried his face in the space between her jaw and her shoulder and hugged her good and tight. After a moment his body relaxed in her arms and when he looked up into her face her smile warmed him down to his toes.

"How 'bout I fix you some breakfast before you go?"

"Pancakes?" he asked, all smiles now.

"Chocolate chip?"

"Yeah! Yeah! Yeah!"

"Okay, chocolate chip it is. You get the stuff ready and I'll find the other boot, okay?"

"Okay, " he said getting to his feet.

"Give me a kiss."

With everything all right again, Kevin dropped a little peck on her cheek and ran down the hall to the kitchen.

Dressed and showered, Sean sauntered into the sunny kitchen and headed straight for the coffee. The warm aroma of fresh pancakes and melted chocolate got his stomach rumbling. He checked the time. No time.

As he poured his coffee he watched Petra leaning against the counter watching Kevin inhale a short stack of pancakes that dripped with maple syrup. He realized that everything he loved was in this room. They were his world. It was a small world, but it was all he needed. Warm and secure. Safe and happy.

"You gonna be able to skate with all that food?" Sean asked, as he dropped two sugars into his travel mug.

"I need the energy, Dad," Kevin replied between mouthfuls.

"Well, that's true," Sean said, sliding down the counter, bumping hips with Petra.

"You need any extra energy, honey?" she said with a smile that said so much more. "You want some breakfast?"

Sean kissed her mouth gently.

"Hey! I'm eating over here," Kevin warned, screwing his face up.

"All right, all right! Eat your food, we're gonna be late," Sean said.

Kevin gobbled up the last few bits of pancake, smearing in the remnants of chocolate and maple syrup that remained on his plate.

"All ready, Dad," he announced, pushing his clean plate away from him.

Sean tossed him the car keys.

"Okay, go start it up and throw in your gear. I'll be right out."

Kevin snagged the keys out of the air and raced for the door where his hockey stick and equipment bag lay waiting.

"Hey! Hey! Hey!" Petra said, stopping Kevin in his tracks. "How about a kiss for the cook?"

"Aw, come on," Kevin whined, making his way slowly back to the counter.

"C'mere, you."

Petra wrapped the boy in her arms and squeezed him tight.

"Have a good practice, Kev."

"I will."

Kevin kissed her cheek and then bolted for the door.

"You see that," she said. "He's forgetting about me already."

Sean leaned into her and slipped his arm around her.

"I won't forget about you," he whispered, kissing her neck, as his hands slid under her shirt.

"Hey!"

"He's outside," Sean mumbled against her neck.

Petra scanned the door and the two windows facing the driveway.

"But he can still come in."

Sean's head came up quickly. "I'll lock the door."

Petra laughed and pushed him off.

"Get out of here, you're going to be late. Put it on your Christmas list."

Sean sighed dramatically as he grabbed his mug and headed for the door.

"But all I want for Christmas is to fill your stocking."

Petra's mouth hung open. "You are filthy, Sheriff!" she said and slapped Sean on the ass as he walked by.

CHAPTER 6

In the parking lot of Danaid's arena, Sean pulled Kevin's hockey bag out of the back of their five-year-old Jeep and closed the hatch. "Remember who you're getting a ride to school with?" Sean asked.

"Ricky's dad."

"And after school Aunt Violet is going to pick you up, okay?"

Kevin slung his bag over his shoulder and said, "Aw, Dad, do I have to stay there tonight?"

"C'mon, buddy, we talked about this. It's just for tonight."

"I know," Kevin said. "But you owe me. Big time. She's not even my real aunt. Plus she's fat."

Sean knew he shouldn't laugh, but he couldn't help it.

"I mean like orca fat," Kevin said. "Free Willy!"

"Come on," Sean said, "Be nice. I could make you sleep in the wood shed."

Kevin beamed, "Could I?"

"No."

Sean stared down at his son as he shifted from foot to foot, struggling with his heavy equipment bag, and watched the boy smile. He had a beautiful smile, and when his eyes found you, you were his. It had been the same with his mother.

"Okay. You do this for me and tomorrow night we'll go down into the city and watch that new movie you wanted to see."

Movies were Kevin's passion and any mention of going into Braden, the next biggest city to the south, to see one on the big screen lit up Kevin's face like a Christmas tree.

" 'They Crawl Again!' "

" 'They Crawl Again'?" Sean asked.

"It's the sequel. I saw the first one at Toby Myers' house, on his satellite. It was awesome. But Petra said I couldn't go."

"Why not?"

"She said that kind of stuff would warp my mind."

"Well, she's probably right," Sean said, watching his son's smile fade.

"She's not even my real mom."

"Hey, enough. You be good tonight."

"Oh, I will. I promise."

"Listen to Violet. And no fat jokes."

"Okay."

"You do that and I guarantee we'll see that movie, okay?"

Kevin threw his arms around his dad and squeezed him tight.

"Thanks, Dad."

Sean waited until Kevin disappeared behind the doors of the arena and then headed over to Station Street.

He pulled into the freshly plowed parking lot of a small squat building where only one other vehicle, an even older Jeep, sat parked in front of a battered metal sign that read:

DANAID SHERIFF DEPARTMENT.

Inside the glass doors were chairs, magazines and a low coffee table giving the place the look of a dentist's office waiting room. And in fact, until six months ago, it was.

The high front desk stood empty, with only a little silver

bell left on the desk blotter attached to a note that read: Ring for Service! Sean slipped past the front desk without ringing the bell and entered the main processing area under a string of green garland. In the cramped little space that the town provided, his office and their only jail cell took up the entire back wall. What remained was dominated by two desks, a main briefing table, a few chairs and some notice boards crammed with local announcements, bake sales, the odd missing person report and Christmas cards that the station received.

As Sean snaked his way through the furniture to his office, the sound of Bing Crosby finishing "White Christmas" leaked out through the building's tinny speakers. He threw his coat into the arms of a chair that faced his desk, sat down and switched on his computer. As Bing began "Silver Bells," a toilet flushed nearby, his office being right next door to the only toilet in the building.

After a moment, Kelly Fike, soon to be Kelly Hanson if the engagement stuck, stepped soundlessly past the glass walls of his office and poked her blonde head into his open doorway. She had the wide, pretty face of a farmer's wife who knows how to bake an apple pie and change the blades on a roto-tiller all with a toddler riding her considerable hip. A hip that had been steadily widening, along with the rest of her, Sean had noticed, since the engagement was announced four months ago.

"Mornin', Sheriff."

"Morning, Kelly," Sean said casting a glance down at her slippered feet, where two fuzzy brown beavers stared up at him, baring their buck teeth. "Think you could put some boots on today, you know, at least look the part?"

"I'm on dispatch today, Sean," she replied, leaving him with a quizzical look. "Where am I going?"

Sean watched her half walk, half slide her way back to the dispatch desk.

Dispatch, Sean thought. *Jesus.* There were about 1500 people in this town during the summer, and fewer than 200 now that winter had rolled in, and only three policemen. Two of whom were in the building. What the hell did they need a dispatch for?

Kelly pulled her slippered feet under her as she shifted her bulk into the chair and grabbed a radio. She squeezed the TALK button and said, "Jordan, come in, over."

There was a crackle of static and then, "I'm here, honeypie," Jordan replied. Sean shook his head. He opened the logbook to last night's entries and found only three. Busy night, he thought. He called for Kelly and she slid into his office stirring what smelled like a mug of hot chocolate. Her mug was yellow, decorated with a smiley face that grinned wildly.

"What's up, Chief?"

"What are these three entries? It says 'tows.' Jordan was out towing people last night?"

Kelly took a sip of her hot chocolate and nodded.

"Yep. First one was Craig Button. Y'know he got that new Land Rover last month and, well, I guess he ditched it over near Peacock Street. Jordan had to pull him out of the ditch."

"So these three entries were people he pulled out of the ditch, not towing them because of traffic violations?"

"Right. They didn't do anything, 'cept get stuck. The second one," she said, shuffling in behind Sean to get a better look at the log, "was, oh yeah, over on Brant Street. Mrs. Wilkes got hung up on a drift. The last one I think was a snowmobile."

"When did we start towing?" he asked, "What about the garage over at the Texaco, what's his name ... Marvin?"

Kelly shrugged her shoulders, "Since Marvin didn't show up for work."

"Well, where is he?"

"I don't know, Sean, no one does. Jordan went over to the garage and it was closed. No answer at Marvin's place either. He lives over on Saturn Crescent in them little townhouses over there." Kelly wrinkled her nose as she mentioned the townhouses as if the very mention of low-income housing offended her delicate sensibilities.

"Beautiful. Winter's just starting and our resident tow truck driver goes AWOL."

"Yup," she said, sliding her way out of his office on her fuzzy brown slippers.

"That's it? You got nothing?"

"Don't look at me," she said. "I can't drive that thing."

"Thanks, Kelly," he replied. "You're all about solutions. I like that about you."

"Hey, that's why you get paid the big bucks."

Sean sat at his desk, thinking about possible tow truck drivers when his eyes found the calendar. His calendar. It sat squarely on the left corner of his desk, just beyond his phone. It was the kind where each square page was a day of the year. The date still read October 21, 2004. The day Kate, Kevin's mother, died.

He hadn't thought about the calendar in a while. In fact he couldn't remember the last time he looked at it. It was odd and a little scary how time had a way of speeding by you while your back was turned, while you were busy with the business of life.

Three years. More than that now. *Had it really been that long?*

He had called home in the middle of the afternoon to find out what was for supper and to chat a little bit. He had no idea that it would be the last time he would speak to his wife. She said that she was tired and going to lie down. She asked if he wouldn't mind picking up Chinese for dinner as she just didn't feel up to cooking. He joked with her about being lazy and she laughed and gave it back to him, as was their way with each other.

When he and Kevin arrived home they found her in the bedroom, asleep. Sean asked Kevin to set the table for dinner and Sean sat on the edge of the bed and kissed her forehead. Her skin was cold.

Dr. Ronald Baron, the town's only year-round physician, performed the autopsy and ruled that Kate had died from an embolism in her brain. Just like that. In an instant, she was gone.

It had taken him a year to even consider removing some of Kate's things from the house. It had taken another to let it happen. And he couldn't do it alone. Violet Monroe and Billy Walters were there to help box things up. But they were there mostly to stop Sean from hiding some of her things and holding on to them. In the end they took everything. Her perfume and jewelry, her shirts and jeans. Even her dresses and skirts, the few that there were. She was never a dress and skirt girl. Not his Kate.

After a while the house stopped smelling like her. And

then one day he found it difficult to remember the sound of her voice. Now, more than four years later, all he had was the stupid little calendar that he just couldn't seem to get rid of.

He picked it up and it was so light, so inconsequential. He found it impossible to rationalize that something like this little package of plastic and paper could have such a hold on him. He rolled his chair to the garbage can in his office and dropped it in.

"There," he said. "Done."

He rolled back to his desk and immediately felt sick. He quickly rolled back and plucked the little calendar from the garbage.

"Not yet," he said just above a whisper. "Not yet."

Thoughts of Petra crept in and he found himself touching the calendar as if it were some weird talisman, some last connection with his dead wife.

"I don't want to forget you," he whispered, "but I think I found someone."

He carefully placed the calendar back on the desk and took the time to straighten it to just the right angle. When he was finished he leaned in close and said, "I think you'd really like her."

Sean left his computer on and grabbed his coat from the chair. He suddenly needed fresh air. He was nearly past the front desk when Kelly called him back.

"Sean, wait!" She whispered into the walkie-talkie, "I'll call you back, honey," adding, "over and out," just to make it official.

"What's up, Kelly?"

"Where're you goin'?" she asked.

"Out to get a muffin."

"Oooh," she moaned. "Mabel's? Are you going to Mabel's?"

"Yeah, probably."

"Could you do me a teencie-weencie little favor?"

"Anything," he said.

"Could you bring me back a piece of bumbleberry pie?" she asked.

"I might not be coming straight back."

"Oh, that's all right, whenever. It's always a good time for pie," she said, giving him a wink with her not-too-bright country grin. "Just tell Mabel it's for me, she still owes me a piece on the house after last week's nightmare. Did Jordan tell you ab—"

"Anything else?" he asked quickly as he inched backwards toward the door.

"Another poster came in for Kevin," she said. "I left it over by the fax machine."

"Where's it from this time?"

"New York, I think, I didn't really look at it."

Sean lifted the sheet from the scarred wood table where the ancient fax machine/copier sat. The picture had been taken from far away but the subject was perfectly centered. He looked to be sitting behind the wheel of a big SUV. He looked straight toward the camera. The details of his face were blurred and softened by the distance, but the menace in his gaze was not. His hooded glare burned right through Sean.

"I don't get why you let Kevin have those things."

"Some kids collect baseball cards, and some kids—"

"Collect Wanted posters of criminals at large?" she finished,

"It's creepy."

"He's a kid. Creepy is cool. I mean, how many kids get to have real copies of police Wanted bulletins?"

"Only the creepy ones."

"You're creepy," Sean snapped.

Kelly stuck her tongue out at Sean and crossed her eyes.

"Beautiful," he said. "Was there anything else before I leave you?"

"Just that Billy Walters called for you a couple times already. Said it was pretty important."

Sean left without another word. Not as important as bumbleberry pie, though. Right, Kelly?

Past the garland hanging in the entranceway, around the front desk he could still hear her as he passed through the double glass doors when she pushed the TALK button on the walkie-talkie.

"Jordan, sweetie, are you there?"

After a squelch of static, "I'm here, honeybear."

CHAPTER 7

The Trading Post was a converted log cabin at the corner of First and Main. A neon OPEN sign hung in the window. Sean tried to find a spot in front of the little store and couldn't. Cars and trucks were lined up on both sides of the street, leaving only one space available. Sean hesitated for a second then said, "Fuck it," and pulled into the handicapped parking space, knowing full well that old Mr. Doogan, whom the spot was for, was down south visiting his sister. He had to remind himself to thank Kelly for that little tidbit, for if nothing else, she was extremely efficient at keeping everyone up to date on the current movements and juicy gossip concerning her fellow locals.

Sean turned up his collar against the wind that seemed equally determined to either bury the Trading Post in snow or blow it off the face of the earth altogether. Huge drifts sailed across the open street to slam against the front of the general store, much to the dismay of Stevie Marshall, the young kid in a ripped leather jacket and blue jeans trying to keep up with the accumulation, shoveling drift after drift off the store-wide front porch.

As Sean passed him he leaned on his shovel, holding a cigarette to his lips with two fingers the color of bone, shivering in the snow that had quickly buried the ankles of his high-tops.

"Looks like it might snow today," Sean said with a grin.

Stevie shot him a black look that could have killed a small

army.

Sean smiled and stamped the snow from his feet on the welcome mat before he slipped inside.

Inside the store was bedlam. In a place where you could get everything from corn flakes to shotgun shells, the line stretched from the cash register to the far west corner of the store, where rental videos were kept. Shoppers pushed their way down the narrow aisles, pulling everything they could into their tiny carts.

As Sean sifted through the crowd waiting impatiently to check out, he spotted Gertie McElroy in Aisle 1. No one knew for sure how old Gertie was, but if he had to guess, Sean would put her around seventy-five at least. Her pale skin was stretched tight against thin bones that gave her the appearance of a delicate marionette. But beneath that globe of pure white hair was a pair of sharp green eyes and a tongue that could cut you to ribbons or warm your heart, depending on her mood, which was unpredictable at best.

When Sean reached her she was trying in vain to sweep up a ripped bag of flour while unruly customers stomped obliviously through her aisle

"For the love of Christ, can't you see what I'm trying to do here, Iris?" Gertie said to a woman in her forties, wrapped in a long fur coat. The woman half-turned to say something, thought better of it and quickly darted down another aisle heading for the frozen foods.

When Gertie spotted Sean wading through the other customers, her pinched expression dissolved.

"Billy's lookin' for ya, Sean."

"That's why I'm here," he replied, as he turned sideways and allowed a mother and her three children to slip by with a cart piled high with groceries. "How you doing?"

Gertie finally gave up sweeping the spilled flour and leaned on the end of her broom. "I'm hanging in there. I'd be a whole lot better if these fool people would just realize that this storm don't mean the end of the world. It's makin' them all skittish, like that damn millennium bug all over again. People are already diggin' themselves in. It happens every year. The days get short and the people get dumb."

Suddenly a big booming voice roared, "Goddammit, people, relax!" For a moment the white noise of mixed conversation and people moving like cattle through the aisles quieted down a couple of decibels as Billy Walters made his way through the mob toward Gertie and Sean.

Billy Walters was a bear who had just begun to gray at the temples. Standing at least six foot five, he was tall and thick, with hands big enough to palm basketballs. He moved with the easy grace of an athlete as he dodged and sidestepped the store's patrons, who clogged every aisle. As always he was dressed in jeans and a white denim shirt with The Trading Post embroidered in gold over the right breast.

"I swear," Billy began, "all these damn people are going absolutely apeshit. Every last one of them. I'm running out of everything and I won't get another delivery until next Thursday, and that's if the trench holds up. That's almost a week with no supplies."

The "trench" was what the locals called the section of road into town. It ran between two sheer walls of rock, a narrow, winding piece of road nearly a mile long, dangerous at the best of times, but during bouts of inclement weather the weary travelers who had to cross it were exposed to falling rocks, high winds and sudden white-out conditions. Every winter it seemed the plows in town made that run every day, sometimes twice, as the road was the only way in or out of Danaid.

"I remember back in '86, the weather got so bad we lost power for a whole week," Sean said. "Had to gather in the church basement and ride it out."

"Well, at least this time we'll be ready," Billy said. "Your girlfriend's been running her little ass off around town getting the word out like the goddamn sky is falling."

"What are you talking about?" asked Sean.

"The Emergency Committee had the church print up flyers to tell folks what to do when they hear the siren and when to come to the church," Billy said. "It was Petra's idea. No one left behind, she said, or something like that. She even arranged a deal with the At Your Service cab company to pick up the old farts like Gertie who might get trapped in their homes."

"And she got Marvin Thompson out walking door to door with the flyers," Gertie said. "She must have a way with words cause that old sonofabitch wouldn't piss on you if you were on fire."

"Marvin, eh," Sean said. Maybe that explained why he'd been unavailable to do his real job, towing. "Have you seen him?"

Gertie and Billy shook their heads.

"His tiny grinch heart probably stopped from the shock of doing a good deed," Gertie said, "You'll find him in a drift somewhere with a fistful of flyers."

"But seriously, Sean," Billy said, "when the bad shit hits, everyone is gonna head over to the church. Now, I've been ordering extra supplies to send over there. If I run out here, people might just go over there and help themselves."

"That's not gonna happen," Sean said.

"You're damn right," Gertie added. "Anybody slides over there with anything but praying on the their mind is gonna catch a load a buckshot between the eyes."

"Jesus Christ, Gertie!" Billy said.

Gertie slapped him hard on the tit, making the big man wince.

"That's for the blasphemy. And for calling me old."

"Fuck me," Billy whispered, massaging his chest. "If people keep buyin' like they are, even if the trench holds I'm gonna have to start rationing. Do you believe that? That's how crazy it is. Like yesterday, Minnie Wilkes comes in here and takes twelve dozen eggs. Then she comes back an hour later and asks if I have anymore! You believe that? What the hell she doing with all them eggs?"

Sean shook his head. "Crazy," he said, but he wasn't surprised. There was nothing a small town liked better than a little excitement. A little hint of danger. With the coming storm they got both.

"Word is that you're looking for me," Sean said.

"Indeed I am. Come with me. Gertie, go help Jessie at the till. Poor girl, they're eating her alive up there."

Sean looked up at the cash register. Billy's fourteen-year-old daughter Jessica looked to be on the verge of tears, trying desperately to replace a roll of receipt tape in the register as the customers, their patience wearing thin, grew louder and louder.

"What about my break?" Gertie asked as Billy guided Sean

toward the rear of the store.

"I'll be right back," Billy called over his shoulder. "Two minutes."

Gertie shook her head and swore under her breath as she stood the broom against the racks and shuffled toward the front of the store.

Billy's "office" was a storeroom stacked high with boxes along three walls, with a little desk, a computer and a narrow kitchen chair.

"Come on in," Billy said, and closed the door behind Sean, dulling the noise of the shoppers. Billy moved to a stack of ketchup boxes and pulled out the bottom one without disturbing the rest of the column. The empty box was placed to the side, revealing a small floor safe. Billy crouched in front of the dial and spun in the combination. He swung the square metal door wide, took out a brown paper package the size of a videotape and tossed it to Sean.

"Came in this morning," he said. "Why'd you send it here?"

"Christ, Billy, you're the only one I know in this town that could keep a secret. If I went to old man Towler's and picked something out, the whole damn town would know before noon. Besides, Towler ain't exactly up on all the latest fashions, y'know."

"Towler's? So it's jewelry. For Petra?"

"No, for you, dummy. Merry Christmas!"

"Up your ass, Sean." Billy closed the safe door and replaced his clever empty ketchup box disguise.

"Still, the box is a little big for an engagement ring."

"Engagement ring? Jesus, Billy, she's only been in town for

what, six months?"

"Yeah, but she's been living with you for four."

There was a silence, then a small, quiet moment where the smiles between friends faded, if only for a moment.

"I'm not even thinking about that right now, Billy."

"I'm sorry, Sean," he whispered. "I should learn when to keep my big mouth shut."

As Sean slipped the package into his coat, Gertie yelled from inside the store, "Time's up. I need my goddamn cigarette!"

Both men looked at each other and smiled ruefully.

Sean tapped on the box through his coat and said, "Thanks, Billy."

"Hey, anytime, but I better get back before old Gertie has a conniption fit. Give my best to Petra and Kevin."

"I will."

Billy opened the office door. All the shoppers were talking at once, fighting over items, complaining about something else, the weather, the lack of selection. Billy looked exhausted as he turned to Sean and suggested that he slip out the back, away from the mob. Sean nodded and headed for the rear delivery door.

"Billy!" Gertie yelled again.

"I'm coming, you crazy old bitch," Billy whispered under his breath.

CHAPTER 8

The Violet House was just north of Mabel's Bakery on Main Street, a small brick shop wedged between the only pub in town, the Ritz, and a thrift shop, The Second Hand Rose. Its large front window showcased the very best in local talent. Portraits and landscapes that did their best to recreate the world around them crowded against one another for the most exposure.

Truth be told, the owner, Violet Monroe, didn't sell very much at all, but she wasn't in it for the money. She lived off her pension and her dead husband's rather large insurance settlement. Apparently, he was crushed at work when a crane malfunctioned and dropped a load of steel, leaving her with a small fortune that guaranteed her a life of relative ease for her remaining years. What little she did sell was to those who mostly came in to gossip or sample the latest batch of cookies that always seemed to be freshly baked and still warm. After a few minutes, or sometimes hours, if the topic was truly juicy, the browser usually went home with a little thumbnail sketch or a cute watercolor for their bathroom or kitchen or den. Violet didn't mind. She enjoyed the company and the conversation, but what she enjoyed most was that the shop allowed her to be around artists.

Whether they were gifted or not, she loved to watch them create, loved the excitement in their eyes as they tried to explain where they got the inspiration, and after, the proud look they gave their work. That was why she ran a painting workshop in the studio behind her shop twice a week, Sunday and Thursday at six PM. At the time she had a class of seven— seven different styles, ages and attitudes, ranging from the dotty old Mrs. Limprey, whose mind wandered mid-painting until her watercolor of a barn somehow ended up being a portrait, to a serious eighth-grader like Josie Tamler, who brought her own special paint, brushes and canvas that her parents had couriered from a professional artist supply firm in Denver.

Of the seven, three were doing fine and might sell some day, if only to relatives, but one was truly gifted, one whom the others studied and watched, whether out of jealousy, respect or wonder. Violet had even caught little Josie tip-toeing past Petra's canvas to sneak a peek.

Beyond the maze of small tables and racks of paintings and prints sat a little counter. It had no cash register, just a cappuccino maker, a plate of cookies, and a small wooden cigar box where Violet kept her change. The store was deserted but as always a small, powerful stereo system piped Eric Clapton, the Rolling Stones or Bob Marley through the small speakers mounted throughout the shop. The morning had started out gray, and more than likely would end that way, and on days like that when Violet needed a little sunshine, Bob always got the call and soon the sweet sound of "No Woman No Cry" drifted on the air.

Behind the counter, through a beaded curtain, lay Violet's own studio. It was a wide-open space where the sunlight fell through skylights and the long narrow windows at the rear of the building. Six easels sat empty at present, the next class two days away. Only one held a painting now.

Violet Monroe stood by the open window, tapping her slippered foot to the beat of the song, whispering the lyrics under her breath as she blew a thin stream of smoke into the outside world.

"Are you ready, yet?" she asked, tapping out a curled length of ash into a glass ashtray.

Petra shifted the painting nervously on the easel, unable to find the center as she bit the end of her thumbnail. Finally, she nodded.

And with that, Violet crushed out the stub of her cigarette and made her way over to Petra, her long metal earrings and her beaded necklaces clinking noisily like miniature wind chimes. Violet always looked, to Petra anyway, like a hip grandmother if there ever was such a thing. She wore heavy sweaters to downplay her considerable size, and today was no exception. Today it was a green and red cable knit, part of her Christmas attire, complete with a team of white reindeer parading around the wide hem. Her face was round, soft and happy, and never without a smile, or a grin. But that was where the whole grandmother image stopped dead.

Her chestnut hair was streaked with white and cut short, leaving her with a messy, spiky, bed-head look that she pulled off quite nicely. She listened to the Rolling Stones, she grew pot in her upstairs attic and she had a tattoo.

Black symbols and characters formed a thin line of script from the base of her hairline at the nape of her neck, to midway down her back. After seeing it, on a rare occasion when Violet had not worn a turtleneck, Petra had asked what the writing meant. Violet gave a far off look, as if remembering some delicious memory, her only reply being that it was a promise she had made long ago, and she had left it at that.

Petra pulled back the cover sheet and unveiled her painting. Violet stood back and studied the work carefully. Her face revealed nothing.

"Jesus," she whispered.

Petra shuffled a little closer to the large woman.

Violet edged forward, almost cautiously, toward the canvas.

"My God, Petra," she said. "Where did you come up with this?"

"You told me to dig deeper. To reveal myself. Well, here I am."

Violet found herself holding her breath, her skin covered in goosebumps. It was nothing more than a bit of canvas and paint, she knew that, but Petra had created something more than a static scene. Much more. Something fluid. The word "alive" spilled over her lips just below a whisper. Violet shook her head.

"Vi?" Petra asked. "Do you like it?"

Violet nodded and tried to smile, but she felt cold and scared for some reason. There was something wrong here, something very wrong. It wasn't something she could put her finger on, but it was there, all around this thing. This *painting*.

"My God, Vi, you're shaking."

Off in the near distance a small bell rang, announcing the arrival of the day's first customer. Violet looked away from the painting and immediately felt better.

"I'll get that," Petra said, moving toward the door.

"No, it's all right, sweetie," Violet replied. She'd do just about anything to be farther away from that painting right now. "It'll probably be Mary Wills, she's been haggling over the Knopfler original for three days straight now."

"The one with the ducks?"

Violet nodded.

"How much does she want to pay?"

"Nothing. Says she's related to the artist in some way. I swear, a couple more days and she's gonna wear me down and she'll leave here wearing that damn thing."

Petra laughed and smiled, but her attention never left the painting.

"Petra, honey, why don't you go on upstairs and find a frame for that, and we'll put it out in the shop. I can't wait till that little snot Josie sees it. She's gonna just shit."

And with that Violet slipped into the shop through the beaded curtain. A few moments later she called out loud enough for Petra to hear, "Hello, Mrs. Wills."

⁂

Petra's smile faded as she reached for her painting with the tips of her fingers. Slowly, she traced the outline of the central figure, the narrow shoulder, the back hunched forward, the sliver of profile left lit by the dim light of a diffused moon. Petra's eyes closed. She swayed slowly like candlelight caught in a breeze.

In an instant the studio, the painting, the entire world was gone, and she was alone in the darkness, swimming among them. She could not see them, but she felt them. They were close. They spoke as one, directly to her, through her, within her. A million voices formed one ancient voice that would not be denied. She gathered its message, slowly collecting, understanding the one word that screamed in her mind. The voice was her own. To herself she whispered the one-word prayer.

Awake.

CHAPTER 9

Norman Conklin found himself channel-surfing for over an hour before he finally killed the television and tossed the clicker onto the sofa. It was no use. *He* was coming and there wasn't a goddamn thing he could do about it. He knew he would come. He knew they would send him. Heartless sonsabitches they were. He should have never taken that picture. He should've said no, I ain't doin' it. But he couldn't and they knew it. And he knew it too. This whole thing was bigger than him. Bigger than the whole town. He needed to take that picture, and he did, and they were pleased. And now *he* was coming.

Finally, he stopped staring into the black middle distance between where he sat and the dead TV. His big blonde lab, Ruby, was already sitting up tall next to the couch. She eyed her owner suspiciously, sensing something amiss but not sure what.

Norman reached down and gave the old dog a good scratch behind the ears. Ruby chuffed and licked his palm. She felt it too, Norman thought. She always could.

Norman wrapped his threadbare housecoat around himself and stepped to the windows that overlooked the driveway. It had begun to snow earlier and now the world was covered in a fresh blanket of white. The wind was constant, blowing drifts of snow across the fields and through the wrought iron fence of the cemetery. Norman let his eyes slide shut as he placed his forehead against the cold window glass. For the most part he pushed their voices away, until they seemed far away, distant, like a radio playing in another room. But today, there was no ignoring them, no tuning them out. Something was happening.

He was coming.

Norman opened his eyes, leaned against the window frame and watched the shadows of skeletal branches and drifts of snow flash across the yard. There were other shadows too, staring up at the bright yellow square of Norman's window. Shadows that belonged to the voices that relentlessly whispered one name in Norman's ear, a name he hadn't heard in over thirty years, a name that brought him back to that first night. The night where his old life ended and his new life began.

The year was 1976. Norman's parents had died in a car accident at the beginning of 1974, leaving him the Danaid cemetery to run. It turned out to be more than Norman could handle. Over the generations, the Conklin family had earned a reputation for class, dignity and respect; however, young Norman seemed committed to tearing that reputation down as quickly as he could.

Since the night the sheriff gave Norman the bad news about his folks, he seemed content to climb inside a whiskey bottle and shut the rest of the world out. During those days he spent the bulk of his time in his bedroom on the second floor. On that particular night, young Norman got himself completely shit-faced by 6:30 PM. Quite an accomplishment, considering his day, which consisted of lying in bed and eating handfuls of Cheerios while he watched an endless parade of game shows.

When Duke (Norman's first dog, who was put down in 1987) barked in the yard outside, he rolled out of bed and kicked an empty beer bottle, sending it spinning across the hardwood toward his bedroom door. He swore as he hobbled over to the window.

Rain had hammered the ground all day and continued into the night. Thick black clouds hovered close to the earth, smothering the dim light of stars. Norman leaned against the window frame and watched the black Mercedes as it crept slowly up the private drive. Headlights swept the two-story brick home, its one white shutter flapping in the wind like a single sail not properly lashed down. On the right side of the house, next to the garage, stood a doghouse, and as the lights swept past, two yellow eyes flashed in the darkness.

The Mercedes pulled to a stop and the engine died. Over the rustling of the trees and the falling rain that slashed at the sleek black car, Duke emitted deep guttural growls as the big German Shepherd inched its way out of its doghouse.

After a moment, the driver's door opened and a huge man wrapped in a heavy overcoat stepped into the storm. He was six foot five at least, with the shoulders of a football player. His face was a sliver of moon beneath his wide-brimmed hat. The interior light in the car revealed a thin pale woman in the back seat. She never turned to look at the house, the growling dog, or even in the direction of the windows. She wore a simple black veil that obscured her features.

As the man stepped toward the house, Duke barked, pulling and tugging on his chain, digging his claws into the muddy ground, begging for the chance to rip into the trespasser. The man turned to the dog and hissed, his breath like smoke in the freezing air. Duke yelped, turned tail and ran back inside his doghouse as if he had been jabbed in the snout with a hot poker.

With the dog silenced, the big man stepped through the puddles toward the front gates of the cemetery. Just before he passed out of sight beneath the eaves, the man looked up. Norman's breath caught in his throat, his heart lurched. He couldn't look away, couldn't move, frozen in that stare. The stranger's face tilted up into the rain, droplets of water gleaming on the pale skin like water on the moon, but it was his eyes that held him, black lifeless eyes that kept him prisoner.

When the man passed beneath the edge of the house and out of sight, Norman kick-started back to life. First a gasp of air filled his lungs, then his heart chugged into a steady rhythm. He stepped closer and pressed his cheek to the cold glass, looking for his night visitor. A moment later the rusted hinges of his garage door groaned as the door was pulled open.

"What the hell?"

Norman left his window and stalked down to his parents' old room where the view of the garage was better. The garage was open.

"Son of a bitch."

Norman couldn't hear much from all the way up on the second floor, but the garage light was on. The big man's shadow flickered and danced over the concrete floor as he searched for something.

Suddenly, the light was extinguished and the mountain wrapped in the black raincoat emerged from the garage holding one of Norman's shovels. Norman's breath caught in his chest.

"Jesus tap-dancing Christ," he whispered fiercely. "Goddamn grave robbers."

The shovel-stealin' bastard slipped quietly across the gravel driveway and through the wrought iron gates of the cemetery. Beyond the gate, the would-be grave robber disappeared and Norman lost sight of him.

"Now we got a problem, Norm," he could hear his father say, as if he were right there in the room.

"You're darn tootin'," Norman replied.

An artillery blast of thunder shook the house. Norman jumped and banged his head off the glass, rattling the window in its frame. He stepped back from the glass and a thought zipped through his mind, leaving a trail of acid that seemed to seep all the way to his stomach, curdling the contents.

Cult.

What if it's some sort of weird cult? Grave robber? In a Mercedes? Not bloody likely. But a satanic, devil-worshipping cult, now they had money. Or at least he had heard they had money. From somewhere, he wasn't sure where. Maybe he heard it on the news, or in town. But the sad truth of it was that either way, rich devil-cult worshipper or grave robber there was a man in the yard with one of his shovels. At—he checked his watch but it was gone—very late, way past visiting hours.

Norman was rooted in place. Should he go down, check it out? For a moment he almost talked himself into taking a step toward the hall and down the stairs. Then he remembered those black, lifeless eyes.

No way in Hell he was going down there half drunk and in his robe, at least not without something to give the big fella pause.

Norman crossed the room to a closet and pulled the chain, snapping a light bulb to life near the ceiling. He reached up over some sweaters and brought down an old Winchester shotgun, a double-barrel job. He cracked the shotgun and inspected the barrels.

"Goddamn devil worshipper. You picked the wrong yard to fuck with," Norman muttered as he spun away from the window to track down his coat and his boots. Dressed and sufficiently armed, he made his way to the side door, the door closest to the cemetery. He grabbed the handle and his hand cramped severely. He cried out as he pried the twisted claw that was once his hand off the doorknob.

"Jesus," he whispered through gritted teeth. He massaged his hand and slowly found he could move his fingers again. He made a fist, shook his head and reached for the doorknob once again.

Don't.

The word flashed across his brain like a Las Vegas neon sign, fifty feet high and blazing red.

Don't go outside, Norman.

But he ignored the command, ripped open the door and stepped out into the rain.

The plastic hood of his pancho covered his head and kept slipping over his eyes. He pointed the shotgun at the ground and moved quickly to the Mercedes parked in the driveway. He told himself that he would talk to the woman first. No reason to make a bad night worse. He hoped it would all be a misunderstanding and that he would be laughing about this very soon. He felt more confident as he approached the car.

"Hello?" he said, as he tried the door handle. The door swung open with a soft click. Norman peered inside and found the back seat empty. He poked his head toward the front and frowned when he found the front seat empty as well. He softly closed the door and turned in a slow circle, looking for the woman he had seen sitting in the back. He scanned the gravel drive, the garage, the cemetery gates and found only darkness and rain. After a final glance around the darkened grounds, he headed toward the gate in the fence.

A moment later, following the swish of the shovel blade as it cut through the sodden earth, Norman saw the big man in a grave. The thin woman stood next to it.

Norman blinked repeatedly as the rain blurred his sight. It couldn't be real, but he saw it. The big man bent over and pulled a body out of the grave—a grave that Norman himself had dug just six months ago. The body looked like a jumble of sticks inside a leather bag. He set the body down carefully beside the grave, and pulled himself out of the hole. Norman watched, crouched between a pair of tombstones. His view through the rain wasn't perfect, but he could clearly see the body lying awkwardly on its side. Its arms were folded behind, the head tilted up to the sky. Rain beat mercilessly on the corpse's papery skin, filling the mouth that hung slightly agape.

Thunder rolled overhead, lightning tore at the boiling clouds. Norman shivered, stuffing his hands deep into his pockets. He watched the corpse, unable to look away, as it was lit in strobes of lightning. The man's pale face looked almost serene, as if he'd been sleeping.

The grave robber reached out for the corpse and its eyes slid open. Norman's breath caught in his throat. The man's eyes were as black as the night. Lightning ripped across the sky and illuminated the emaciated face. It was no mistake, no trick of the light. The corpse's eyes were open and they had found Norman.

Even hidden well back behind a row of tombstones, Norman felt like he was naked in the middle of Times Square. The man's eyes rooted him in place, bored through him. Norman struggled to move, crawling backward through the wet grass, knocking over plastic vases of flowers and pictures left by the graves. He clumsily got to his feet and turned, walking straight into the veiled woman. The shotgun slipped from his hand as he stopped dead. She stood as silent and as still as a stone angel.

"Don't run, Norman," she whispered.

Norman ran.

The big grave robber blocked the easiest path back to the house, but Norman knew another haven. He took off through the tombstones, sticking close to the tombs that offered the best cover. He had run this cemetery as a kid, playing hide-and-seek, but that was a long time ago and at thirty-eight he was soon out of breath, his belly bouncing under his poncho, his chest wheezing like an asthmatic's. He had to get away, had to keep moving, it wasn't far now.

The shed was no more than a closet near the east corner of the cemetery, a storage shed with a rake, a shovel, bags of weed and feed and an old bleach jug that Norman used to piss in when he was working out in the yard. If no one was in the cemetery he'd piss just about anywhere, but when people were grieving a couple of rows down, one had to be a little more discreet.

He moved a few heavy bags away from the corner and crept in behind them. He found a small, rusted spade and clutched it in his right hand. He took a few practice swings and nodded at the efficiency of his makeshift weapon. He was ready. He crouched behind the bags of fertilizer and not for the last time cursed himself for being so fool stupid to drop his own shotgun. He squeezed the handle of the spade and listened to the rain beat a rhythm on the tin roof. He was prepared to wait all night, to wait forever as long as he never had to see those people again.

The shed was old and the construction shoddy. The planks that formed the walls had split and shrunk over the years, leaving gaps between them. Flashes of lightning sent blades of light into the shed, illuminating the cluttered interior. The dark figure passed by the rotted wall to Norman's left. He squeezed his eyes shut and prayed to whoever might be listening to allow him to wake up from this nightmare. Waves of thunder crashed overhead and Norman opened his eyes.

He turned toward the wall at his back where a crack at eye level gave him a one-eyed view of the cemetery. The bare branches of the trees shook in the wind. He strained to find some clue as to his pursuers' location. Perhaps they had given up. It was a terrible night, and even if he were to tell anyone what he saw, who would believe him? He hated the ammonia-and-urine smell of the shed. He hated the way his wet clothes clung to his skin. He was cold and miserable and scared and he wanted to go home. How long had he been out here? How long since he had seen the shadow pass by the crack in the wall? He set down his rusted spade and turned again to the crack at his back and stared into a black eye set in a face cut from ivory.

Before he could move or scream or even take a breath, a fist thundered through the tiny crack in the wall and grabbed the front of Norman's coat. The giant pulled his fist back and dragged Norman with it. Planks of wood tore apart, showering splinters over Norman's pathetic form as he lay curled in a tight ball on the wet grass.

"On your feet," the man growled, as he grabbed Norman by the scruff of his neck and wrenched him up off the ground. Norman stood trembling, covered in wood dust, as blood streamed from his nose and forehead.

The woman stepped from the shadows of a nearby tomb. As she approached, Norman felt in his bones the shroud of cool air that surrounded her. A coil of terror thrashed in his guts, kicking and snapping until he felt like he was going to throw up or pass out. But he was not afraid of death: at that moment, he would welcome it. Swift and clean, in an instant he would be far from here, far from this woman whose presence made his skin crawl and the blood in his veins run cold. Norman had always heard that there were worse things than death, and as the pale woman wrapped in black whispered through the space between them, he knew in his bones that this woman knew them all by heart.

"Norman Conklin," she said, "you were warned to stay inside your home, were you not?"

Norman nodded weakly.

"Speak up, Norman." Her voice was as smooth as her skin, as if it were cured over time. Her age was a mystery. She looked to be in her thirties, but her dark, half-lidded eyes betrayed her for a woman far older.

"I ... Yes, I was."

She stepped closer, her breath cold on Norman's chin.

"But you had to see, didn't you?" she whispered, a coy smile playing on her lips. "You had to see it all, didn't you,

Norman?"

Norman whimpered, "Yes, ma'am" and sobbed. He shook in his boots. Her eyes searched his face, drinking up his suffering and fear. "Then you shall see everything."

She slid her smooth hands over Norman's cheeks and lowered his face until she could place her full lips over his eyes. Her lips were soft and cold as she kissed each eye, one after the other, and when she was finished she whispered, "Sleep now." Norman slipped from her grasp and crumpled to the ground in a pile of rags like a marionette whose strings had been suddenly severed.

Later, when the air had frozen and the rain turned to sleet, Norman awoke curled in a tight ball, nearly frozen to the muddy ground. He struggled to his feet. His body ached, especially his nose, which he had broken when he crashed through the thin wall of the shed. For a moment he saw her, standing in a pool of shadow. His heart raced. He peered into the darkness, but she was only the ragged remains of a shrub that had survived the winter. He turned on his heel and headed back toward the house.

As he crossed the driveway through the drizzling sleet he thought he saw the shadow of a man out of the corner of his eye, but when he turned, the shadow was gone. He stood there a moment, scanning the darkness, until the aches and pains and the freezing wind chased him inside toward the warmth of the house.

He closed the front door and secured the deadbolt. As he peeled the soaked poncho from his shoulders he heard his name whispered directly behind him. He spun in place, one arm in, one arm out of his poncho, and saw an old woman standing at the bottom of his staircase.

She was just under five feet tall, graying brown hair pulled into a tight bun at the back of her head. Her plump little hands were clasped together beneath the wide bosom of her favorite flower print dress. She smiled nervously when she saw him and whispered his name again, tears rolling over her cheeks.

Norman's mother took a small step toward him and he recoiled. Dead. She was dead. She *is* dead.

"Yes," she replied in his mind. "I am dead. But I'm not gone. I'm always with you. Now you can see that."

And that's when it hit him. One of the million things that were worse than death. The veiled woman had given him sight.

"Look around you," his mother said, pointing to the windows at the side of the house that looked over the cemetery. "A whole world beneath the one you know."

Norman stepped to the windows and stared through the rain and through the black gates of the cemetery. He waited. Soon there was a twitch, a shadow moving among the plots, and then another. Wraiths, young and old, stepped through the long rows of headstones, walking toward the house, matching his stare with their own.

"Don't be afraid," his mother whispered.

Norman sank to the floor, closed his eyes and screamed.

CHAPTER 10

The Danaid cemetery spread over acres of softly rolling hills. The entire area was surrounded by a high black wrought iron fence that was heavily spiked. Bishop piloted his Ford Bronco through the deepening snow of Quaker Road, scanning the plots through the gaps in the fence as he whipped by. He drove past the roadway that led into the cemetery and turned into the next driveway, which wound its way up a small hill to a house that sat back and to the left, partially hidden by a screen of trees.

He found a small barn-style garage at the end of the driveway. The heavy wooden door was pushed open on its track, allowing Bishop to pull inside.

Bishop closed the garage door and trudged through the drifting snow to the side door. From an interior pocket he withdrew a small wallet of thin tools used to pick locks, but he tried the doorknob and it turned in his hand.

"Small towns," he whispered.

The back door led to a mudroom where the heat and the smell of coffee and bacon began to thaw the chill out of his bones. He passed through the kitchen and stepped into a sparsely decorated living room.

Sean scribbled his name at the bottom of a file and slipped the form into the OUT basket. He gathered up his coat, logged off his computer and switched off the lights to his office.

"You outta here?" Kelly asked, tossing a tennis ball against the far wall and catching it easily in her baseball glove.

"Yes, ma'am. I'll see you Monday."

"Okay, Sheriff."

Sean was just past the front desk when he turned and said, "And Kelly ..."

"Yeah?"

"No calls tonight, okay? Short of Armageddon, you two just handle it, okay?"

"Gotcha," she said, tossing the ball at a faded poster of Smokey the Bear.

Outside, Sean dusted a few fresh inches of snow from his Jeep while he waited for the interior to heat up. When all was clear he slid behind the wheel. So far so good, he thought. He pulled out of the station house parking lot smiling.

Bishop soon found what he was looking for in a small office off the main hall. Displayed on the wall was a diagram of the Danaid Cemetery, the plots numbered from 1 to 1905. Along the bottom edge of the diagram he found the funeral home's address, phone, and fax number along with its web address.

The computer sitting on the desk was already on. Its screen saver was a picture of Norman and his dog, a yellow lab. Norman was dressed in fishing attire, complete with the vest of a million pockets and the floppy hat studded with pins and hooks and lures. And even though time and age had softened the young man's features and replaced his black hair with gray, Bishop could still see the young man he saw over thirty years ago in that smiling face.

Bishop moved the mouse and the smiling couple disappeared, exposing the desktop icons. The icon labeled

Danaid Cemetery led him to a searchable web site. The cursor blinked. For a moment Bishop's fingers hovered over the keys. Finally, he typed in a name he hadn't spoken for thirty years and pressed ENTER. He didn't speak the name, for that would dredge up too many memories. Memories that should remain buried. Or maybe it wouldn't. What if he spoke the name, and it meant nothing to him? Just another name without a past. A void. What would be worse?

Almost instantly the request came back and for a moment the screen was black. Slowly, as the file downloaded, the screen filled with three different articles that included the name he had entered. Apparently the cemetery web site was cross-referenced with the local newspaper, the *Danaid Daily*. He clicked on the last one and read the short obituary. Beneath the obituary a line read: Danaid Cemetery plot number 1879. The listing came with a printable map detailing the location of the cemetery and the grave. Bishop elected to print the map and Norman's printer ground to life.

When the map was printed he exited the program and the house.

Sean steered his Jeep through the narrow covered bridge while the stoplight was still green. He switched on his headlights and illuminated the interior of the bridge, revealing the rotting boards and shaking timbers as he bounced over the uneven planks that hadn't been replaced since the town built it about a hundred years ago.

When he emerged on the other side, the road curved to the right as it wound around the cemetery. The black wrought iron fence stood out in sharp contrast to the snow. He had always thought of the cemetery as a particularly creepy place, especially in the fall after the knotted and gnarled trees lost their leaves. But today, with the snow covering everything in a deep blanket of white, even this place looked beautiful.

Bishop stepped through the plots, through the heart of the cemetery. He moved quickly as the wind rode up the rolling land to meet him, powdering his coat and needling his face with clouds of snow and ice. At a tall twisted tree, he consulted his map again and then turned left, following the line of headstones toward the northwest corner. Here the plots were much older, their names rubbed smooth by weather and time.

After one quick backtrack he found the stones he was looking for. They were higher than the ones nearest them, standing tall. Two tall stones turned inward toward a smaller one. He brushed away the snow and read the names for the first time in over thirty years.

Bishop could feel him before he saw him. He looked to his left and saw Oliver Dannon leaning on a nearby crypt.

"I saw you pull in," Oliver said, "I thought you might find your way up here."

Sean dropped the Jeep into fourth and climbed the crest of the hill. The iron fence whipped by and the tombs were a blur, but a smear against the white landscape made him turn.

The large man was dressed in a leather car coat, black gloves and jeans. His dark hair was cut short and pushed forward over a face that was as pale as the surrounding snow. He didn't know why he stared at the man, gazing intently at the graves; it wasn't in his nature to be prying or rude, but something about the man put him off. His foot eased up off the accelerator.

The man's head snapped up and he stared straight at Sean. It might have been a trick of the failing light, it might have been the glare off the snow, but Sean could have sworn that the man's eyes were silver, frosted like chips of glass. Sean couldn't look away. The encounter couldn't have lasted more than three seconds, but he was a mile away from the cemetery before he realized that he had been holding his breath.

He hit the brakes and steered his Jeep to the side of the road. He reached for the Wanted poster sitting on the passenger seat and said, "You gotta be shitting me."

He made a u-turn and headed back toward the cemetery.

"Jordan, where are you?" Sean barked into the radio.

After a pause, Jordan's voice. "I'm on my way to Duke's—I mean, going to get something to eat. For dinner. For my dinner break."

"Shoot pool on your own time, Jordan," Sean said. "I need you at the cemetery right now. I'll be parked outside."

"What's going on?"

Sean slowed to a stop outside the cemetery gates and killed the engine.

"I don't know. Maybe nothing. Just get over here."

"On my way."

Oliver found Bishop's gaze. "It seems things have progressed faster than we anticipated. We don't have a lot of time. She's awakened others."

"How many?"

"At least five so far. Maybe more."

Jesus Christ. Five. And those five would awaken more

and the chain would continue until there were no humans left in Danaid. Until *they* were everywhere. Until they were everyone.

"Have your wraiths found the nest?"

In every city that the Ministry had found them, they had found a nest. It was usually close, or even within the target city limits, and usually underground.

"She's made her nest in the Monk's Head Mine, about ten minutes outside of town."

Oliver drifted away and blended into the shadows. Bishop remained staring at the three tombstones in silence.

Sean stared into the cemetery. He pulled his pistol from his shoulder holster and checked that it was loaded. His heart skipped a beat as it always did when he handled his weapon. He felt himself breathing faster. He put it away.

When Jordan finally got there, Sean was out of his Jeep before the wheels of Jordan's ride stopped spinning. Jordan looked excited and scared.

"What's going on?"

Sean handed Jordan the Wanted bulletin.

"He's here," Sean said.

Jordan read the bulletin and his complexion dropped from pale to ashen.

"You sure?" Jordan whined. "It says he killed a family outside New York City. A whole family, Sean."

"I know."

Jordan paused for a moment, a little out of breath. "Jesus. What's he doing here?"

"I don't know." Sean drew his weapon and Jordan's eyes

popped. "Come on. Take out your gun, Jordan. But keep your safety on, for Christ's sake. I don't want to get shot in the back out here."

Jordan did what he was told, looking like he was ready to puke. His weapon hung limply in his hand.

Sean led his deputy through the cemetery gates and into the parking lot. Only Norman Conklin's piece of shit pickup truck sat parked in front of the garage at the end of the long drive.

Scanning as he went, Sean moved quickly. He made his way through the plots up to the older section of the cemetery. He passed a crumbling archangel and a moss-covered tomb. He reached the top of the slope and surveyed the area.

He registered only movement at first. Then he saw the black coat like a shadow pass behind a stand of trees. He grabbed Jordan's shoulder and pointed.

"Head off to the left and make your way back up to me. Flush him toward me."

Jordan nodded, not taking his eyes off the shadow down below.

"You okay, Jordan?"

Jordan nodded again and was off. Sean cut to the right and headed toward the stand of trees, and the shadow they were trying to hide.

His heart racing, Sean stepped as quietly through the snow as he could, but a deaf guy could have heard him crunching through the hard pack a mile away. He moved around an ornately decorated crypt and found what he was looking for.

The man had his back to him, standing stock still in front of three tombstones. From the Jeep he had looked much bigger, broader. Now that Sean was up close and not whipping by at fifty miles an hour, the long black coat hung off the man's narrow frame. His shoulders were slumped and rounded. About twenty feet in front of the suspect, Jordan picked his way through the graves. Sean stepped closer and raised his weapon.

"Freeze! Police!"

The man in the black coat jumped and jerked like he was jabbed with a hot poker. His hands shot into the air and he spun toward Sean's voice. He lost his footing and fell into the snow on his ass, his arms still in the air.

"Jesus Christ, Sean!" Norman Conklin yelled. "What are you trying to do to me? Give me a heart attack?"

"What are you doing here?" Sean asked.

"What am I doing here? I live here. What the hell are you doing here?"

Sean scanned the grounds all around him and suddenly felt a little stupid. Embarrassed even. Jordan slipped his gun into his holster and dragged out a cigarette. Norman brushed snow from his pants and coat, all the while giving Sean the stink eye.

"I was driving by and I thought I saw someone out here in the yard."

Norman nodded.

"Congratulations. You found me."

"Not you. Someone else."

"Someone else?" Norman asked. "Who, Sean?"

Sean took another long look around the graveyard.

"Sean?"

All he saw were graves and crypts and the darkness closing

in.

"No one, Norman," he answered. "I guess, no one."

CHAPTER 11

Sean sang along with the Rolling Stones at the top of his lungs as they grinded through "Paint it Black." He chopped vegetables and peeled potatoes; he even made biscuits from scratch. Tonight he could do no wrong. Everything was turning out as it should. In forty minutes, Petra would be home and his plan would be complete.

He turned toward the spice rack for a little paprika and nearly bumped into the woman standing in his kitchen. He let out a quick shout and stumbled back.

"Jesusfuckingchrist!"

The woman, wrapped in a woolen parka, made a pained face and tried to say something but the music drowned her out. Sean held up a finger and scrambled for the remote to the stereo. He tossed aside bags of produce and cookbooks as the woman peeled off layer after layer of outerwear until she was down to a cable knit sweater and jeans. She held her coat, scarf and gloves to her chest. A small puddle of melting snow grew at her feet. Sean found the remote under a box of pasta and killed the volume.

"I'm so sorry, Sean," Nancy Tinsel began. "I didn't mean to scare you. I tried calling, but no one answered, so I just came over. I knocked, but with the music so loud …"

"It's okay, Nancy, I just—wow! You scared the shit out of me."

Nancy gave up a weak smile and ran a nervous hand through a tangle of red hair, pulling it back over her ear.

"Can I get you something to drink? Coffee? Something stronger?"

"No, no thank you, Sean. I don't know why I came over, I'm just, well ..."

Sean took a sip of his beer and asked, "What is it?"

"Well, you know Floyd takes Randy out to the Monk's Head Mine every year to go hunting."

Sean nodded. "Sure."

"Well, they left three days ago and they haven't come back."

"When were they due?"

"This morning. They always come back the same time, for Randy's birthday. He has a party and everything."

"Well, they're probably just waiting out the storm. Weatherman says we're supposed to get hit pretty hard for the next few days."

"Still, I'm worried."

And she looked it. Nancy had always been a happy, pleasant woman with an easy smile. Tonight she looked like she had aged ten years. "If they were going to be late they would have radioed."

"Well, of course you're worried, but really, you shouldn't be. Floyd knows these parts better than anybody."

Nancy started to cry. Her eyes squeezed shut, her lips trembled.

"Oh, Sean, would you ...?"

Sean set down his beer bottle and took her by the shoulders, guiding her gently to a kitchen chair, and sat her down.

Sean's eyes squeezed shut, because he knew what was coming. *Not tonight. Jesus, any time but tonight.*

"Would I what?" he asked and winced.

"Take a ride out there to Monk's Head," she said, tears welling in her already red eyes. "Look for my family. Please?"

Sean's shoulders slumped.

"Please ..." she whispered. "I would go myself, but I have to get back to watch Samantha."

"Who's there now?" Sean asked.

"Trisha Evans, she lives across the way, but she's got dance class and can't stay," she replied, scanning the wall clock. "I have to get back."

Nancy got to her feet and pulled on her coat and the rest of her gear. When all of her red hair was tucked beneath her toque she edged toward the door.

"Sean, I'm sorry to ask you to do this, but I'm just so scared. This hasn't happened before. Ever."

"It's okay. I'll go. I'll go right now and take a look."

Nancy grabbed him with her mittens and kissed him quickly on the cheek.

"Thank you. Thank you so much."

"No problem."

"And you'll call me?"

"The minute I'm back. I swear."

Sean walked her to the door where he watched her climb onto her snowmobile and spark it to life. After a quick wave she disappeared into the swirling snow.

Back inside the kitchen he watched as all of his culinary creations rapidly turned to shit. Sauces boiled over, biscuits were ready to smoke. He turned off all the power and swore. Repeatedly. He then ripped a sheet from a scratch pad and scribbled a quick note to Petra. He left it under the bottle of wine on the counter.

Ten minutes later he stepped into his garage wearing a backpack containing, among other things, emergency first aid, food, water and extra bandages. He wasn't sure what he would find out there but he wasn't going empty handed. And just to be safe, he slipped his 9mm Beretta into a front pocket of his coat.

He pulled the tarp from his snowmobile and cranked the engine. In a cloud of oil and gas, he sped out of the garage into the storm, heading due north toward the Monk's Head Mine.

CHAPTER 12

Sean followed the path of the abandoned train tracks through the forest all the way to the mine. It was a longer route than if he weaved through the trees, but the tracks were generally clear, and he wasn't in the mood to do any backtracking. He had been out there for twenty minutes, and he was already freezing. His face was numb and his hands felt like they were welded to the handlebars.

When he finally broke through the trees, the mining office loomed high above him. Broken windows, the crumbling structure built right into the mountain, the place had everything you needed for a good old-fashioned haunted house. Not to mention the ghosts of all the men who were buried here in a cave-in that finally shut the place down in '66.

He pulled into the train tunnel and cut the engine. For a moment the grumbling of the engine rebounded off the brick walls. He climbed off the snowmobile and walked around a bit, working out the kinks in his thighs and back.

He snapped on his flashlight and found the stairs that led to the raised platform of the loading dock and headed toward the only entrance on this side, a pair of double steel doors. If they weren't open, he'd have to trek back through the snow to the front of the building. He reached the doorknob and pulled.

"Fuck," he said when they didn't budge. He pulled again and the door creaked. He put his foot against the frame and pulled again. The door opened about six inches with a tortured groan. He took a better grip, planted his foot on the frame and pulled again. The door opened three more inches and froze. After a few more good pulls he realized that the door just wasn't up to moving, so he held his parka tight to his body and squeezed inside.

He found himself in a short corridor that was as wide as the double doors. He stepped to the end of the corridor where, through another set of doors, he found a large empty storeroom. Steel racks bolted to the floor stood bare. His footsteps sounded like gunshots on the concrete floor as he stepped through the empty racks to a single door at the far wall, the cone of light bobbing ahead of him in the dark, revealing the area twenty feet at a time.

Next he passed through what must have once been the office core, a large, glassed-in room divided by partitions where abandoned cubicles gathered cobwebs, snow and the odd piece of garbage. At the base of a spiral staircase he shone his light around in a circle and called out to Randy and Floyd. Only his echo replied. He started climbing the spiral staircase.

When was he going to learn to say no? Just say no. He could have. He could have said, "Nancy, I'm sorry, but it will have to wait until morning." But no, he didn't say that, and now he was climbing a spiral staircase in the dark in an abandoned mine looking for two grown men who probably weren't here. They were probably at home right now with their feet up, having a beer.

The staircase shifted under him. Sean let out a little squeal and gripped the handrail. "Son of a bitch," he spat. The staircase settled and he moved on. They fucking better be up here, he thought.

At the top of the staircase he passed through the double

doors of an ancient conference room. He swept his light from side to side, illuminating little drifts of snow and bits of garbage. The next room was finally a winner.

He recognized Floyd's gear, and even if he hadn't, Floyd had written F. Tinsel on almost everything. A little habit left over from Floyd's Army days. There was a halogen lamp, an unrolled sleeping bag, a camp stove. Pretty much all of Floyd's gear he thought. Just no Floyd. And no sign of Randy.

This was starting to get serious. Now he knew at least they had been here and then left in a hurry. And it would have to be some kind of major hurry for Floyd to leave all his gear here. If there was one thing he knew about Floyd Tinsel it was that when it came to his gear he was almost obsessed. Everything had to be clean. Everything had to be put away and stored in a certain way and you certainly never, ever, left your kit like this in a haphazard pile.

Sean swept his light over the rest of the room and found the coat next to a door marked Stairs. He had teased Floyd about the yellow coat every chance he got because he knew that Nancy had picked it out for him. Safest color he could wear, she said.

He picked the coat up. It was shredded, nearly ripped in two up the back. He dropped the coat, spun around and swept the light over the room behind him. Nothing had moved. Everything was right where he had found it.

He turned back to the metal door and eased it open. Dust motes danced in the white beam of his flashlight.

"Floyd?" he yelled into the darkness. "Randy?"

His voice fell through the hundred feet of rock tunnel to the ground floor and died. Are you really going down there? he asked himself. Really?

Nothing added up. No snowmobiles outside, but here was Floyd's kit and seriously damaged coat. If he was somewhere in the wilderness that nearly surrounded the town, he was doing it without gear or coat. Not bloody likely. Not when the wind chill was dropping the temperature into the minus twenties. No, something had happened, and it happened right here. Whatever it was cut the coat off his back.

Sean made his way down yet another staircase. This one spiraled into a darkness so thick it seemed to choke the air from Sean's lungs, worse with every step. When he reached the bottom, he listened. The silence was unbelievable. There was no wind, no creaking structure. It felt like being buried alive. Silent. Dark. Suffocating.

A footstep shuffled in the dark. He moved toward the sound, swinging his light up, but found nothing but rock wall.

"Floyd? Randy?"

He kept moving. His light passed from left to right. Not for the first time he asked himself, What am I doing here? He had no answer other than the fact that he knew, if the roles were reversed, Floyd would be down here for him. "Yeah right," he whispered. "He would've waited until morning, got a search party out here, done it the right way, instead of coming down here like some half-cocked one-man army."

Sean's light slipped through the doorway of a small room to his right and an eye stared up at him. He jumped. His heart lurched in his chest and sweat popped out all over his body. He took a tentative step back and stared hard at the object on the floor.

The object was actually *objects*, a pile of them, whatever

they were, bits here and there of all shapes and sizes. Some were as small as a couple inches square, others at least a foot long, and all were dirty gray and cracked. They resembled pieces of wax that had been peeled off something. Something big.

Sean played the light over the piece with the eye and the light passed right through it. He reached for it and it disintegrated at his touch, falling through his fingers like sand. He rubbed his fingers together and the ash left an oily residue on his skin. It made his skin feel cold and slightly numb. He quickly swiped his hand on his jeans and stood up.

That's when he heard it, a low chittering sound, an organized rattle of bones. It sent goose bumps all over his skin. Sean jumped and his heart kicked into overdrive. It was time to leave. He had done all he came to do. He would organize a search party in the morning, like he should have done in the first place, and get the hell out of here double-quick.

The sound was closer the second time. Sean picked up his pace. By the time he hit the spiral staircase heading back up into the office, he was running. He didn't care about stealth, all he wanted was to be up out of the darkness and into the fresh air outside.

Whatever made the horrible sound was gaining on him, getting closer with every breath he took. His heart hammered in his ears. He put one foot in front of the other and pulled himself up the stairs with his hands. Below him something heavy hit the metal staircase. The structure shook beneath him, groaning as its frame twisted. If he looked over his shoulder he would see the clouds of breath from whatever was after him, but if he stopped to glance over his shoulder, the race would be over.

He reached the top of the stairs, bolted through the office doorway and slammed the metal door closed behind him. Something slammed into it and shook the entire wall. That horrible rattling sound grew louder and made his skin crawl. He scanned the cluttered room for something to wedge the door closed and spotted Floyd's collapsible metal cot leaning against the wall. Keeping his left hand around the doorknob he reached the cot with his right. He rammed the folded cot under the twisted doorknob and wedged the exposed metal edges into the floor. It wouldn't last forever, but it would buy him time. He stepped away from the door and the frame shook as it was hammered from the other side. Claws scraped across the metal.

The door was about to come off its hinges.

His head spinning, Sean ran through the door into the next room. Nausea rolled through him. This sweet simple world of his, with its small-town charm, was suddenly foreign and alien and very dangerous. He ran through the chain of rooms, followed by the sound of enraged shrieks and thrashing at the metal door.

What breed of monster had found them?

CHAPTER 13

Minnie Wilkes was nearly set. She had the teakettle boiling. She had her favorite little sugar cookies. Only eight, no more, no less. She had to ration, had to watch her sugar, or so Dr. Baron had warned her. But at eighty-two, this retired schoolteacher was, at least in her own mind, beyond rationing. And she had told him so. If she wanted her sugar cookies, she was gonna eat the whole box and that's that. But to be honest, any more than eight gave her serious stomach cramps.

The kettle sang and she poured boiling water into her oversized mug, dropped in two teabags and she was set.

She took her plate and mug into the front porch and set them down on the side table. All she needed now was some action.

She took a swig of her strong tea and a bite of a delicious sugar cookie and waited. The entire length of her porch was windows that provided her a clear view of Main Street all the way to the corner of Cross Street to the left and all the way to the trench to her right.

She picked up her binoculars and scanned the neighborhood. She was the eyes of the street. Normally, at least during the warmer months, things up her way were a little more lively: people leaving for work and school, delivery trucks coming in from Braden, the next town over. But now with winter rolling in and the population cut to the bare bones, she was lucky if she saw someone get caught in the snow. She tried to pick out the houses that were still occupied. There were only three that she knew for sure, and their windows were dark.

She took another sip of her tea and ate a few cookies and wondered idly if there was anything on the television. Her son had recently bought her a satellite dish for her birthday. Now all her favorite shows were at her fingertips.

Her bulldog, Wrinkles, lifted his head. He had been so quiet she was a little startled. She hadn't even heard him enter the porch. A low growl began to build in his throat.

"What is it, Wrinkles?" she asked.

Wrinkles stepped toward the windows and stared intently into the street. Minnie peered into the street too, following the dog's gaze, but she couldn't see a damn thing.

"What are you looking at, you crazy mutt?"

Then she heard it, the low whine of a snowmobile, coming fast. It came from town and whipped noisily past the porch. Wrinkles lost his mind. He ran to the window and, paws up on the glass, barked his balls off.

Goddamn Randy Tinsel. What was he doing up here at this time of night?

Seconds later one of the town's two snowplows lumbered up the street. But the snowplow wasn't plowing. Its blade was raised and it wasn't spreading salt either. The heavy truck cut a path through the six inches of snow as easy as you please up to the trench. When it was about twenty feet into the trench the plow cut hard to the left and then reversed. It ended up parked smack dab in the center of the road, easily blocking off both lanes of traffic.

"Now what the hell is he doing, Wrinkles?"

The dog had no answers.

The driver's door opened and Floyd Tinsel dropped from

the cab.

"And would you look at that. No jacket in that God-awful cold out there. No common sense if you ask me, Wrinkles. Man goes out there without the proper attire he only has himself to blame. He won't get no sympathy from me, no sir."

He moved with purpose to the gas tank, unscrewed the cap and let it fall into the snow.

Randy Tinsel waited patiently on his skidoo, parked a good fifteen feet away from the snowplow, engine running.

Minnie grabbed her binocs without taking her eyes off the scene outside and watched as Floyd Tinsel wedged some sort of cloth into the gas tank of the plow.

"Holy sweet mother of God," Minnie whispered.

With a brass Zippo lighter, Floyd lit the cloth hanging from the snowplow's gas tank and ran. He hopped on the back of Randy's snowmobile and Randy gunned the engine, tearing out of there.

The explosion lifted the big truck off the ground. It bucked like a living thing. Fire and snow and steam shot upwards and north and south through the trench.

Minnie thought her windows were going to blow out like in the movies, but they held. The house trembled beneath her feet. She could hear falling rocks but she could see nothing. When the smoke and steam had dissipated somewhat, the mouth of the trench reappeared.

Suddenly the friendly northern town where everyone knew everyone else had become a prison. The one road that ran in and out had been effectively blocked.

They were trapped.

Deputy Jordan Hanson leaned over the pool table and stared down the end of his cue as he lined up his next shot. The shirtsleeves of his tan deputy's uniform were rolled up high on his arms. His radio and revolver rested on a nearby table among the empty beer bottles and a tin ashtray overflowing with butts.

Andre Taluc, a long and lanky remnant of the eighties, was a permanent fixture at the local arcade and pool hall, dressed as always in some ancient concert t-shirt and ripped jeans.

Jordan whistled through his teeth as he leaned over his next shot. His short, compact body gave him the look of a baby-faced bull. A cigarette dangled from his lips as he took his shot. Andre sipped his beer as he followed the cue ball through two banks to finally tap the eight ball into a far corner. When the eight ball dropped, he finished his beer, dug out a crumpled ten spot and tossed it on the table. Jordan snatched up the ten and held it tight to his nose, breathing deeply.

"I hope that bill smells like my ass," Andre said, pulling on his jean jacket.

"Nope," Jordan replied. "Smells like victory."

Andre lit another cigarette and smiled weakly.

"Come on, one more game," Jordan said, racking the balls into the triangle.

"Don't you work for the police force or something?"

"Why? Does it show?" Jordan said. "Come on, Andy. I'll give you the break."

As Andre thought about the offer, Jordan signaled to the waitress, who was Andre's mother, for two more beers.

"Come on, double or nothing."

Andre didn't have to think about it long. After all, where the hell else did he have to go?

"Give me that fucking thing," Andre replied, as he pulled the cue from Jordan and lined up the break. "You should arrest yourself for hustling," he said.

As Jordan paid for the two beers, his radio crackled to life. "Jordan, honey, you there?"

"You better get that, Jo-Jo," Andre said and smashed the cue ball for the break.

Jordan scooped the radio from the table. "I'm here, Kelly, go ahead," he replied.

"Mrs. Wilkes called, said there was something funny about the trench up by her."

Jordan watched as Andre moved around the table eyeing up his next shot.

"What is it?"

"I don't know, she said something about an explosion. You know how she is. She's called five times already asking when we were coming out. You better go out and check, just to be sure, okay, honey?"

Jordan winced as Andre dropped his third shot in a row; the next two were easy, then the eight ball. Andre could barely stop grinning.

"Jordan? You there?"

"Okay, sweetie. I'll be out there soon."

A half hour later and twenty bucks lighter, Jordan passed St. Patrick's church and made a left on Main Street to head out to the south end of town where Minnie Wilkes lived. Her house was the last on the road before the trench.

She stood in her front window, wrapped to her throat in a green robe, her long white hair spilling over her thin shoulders and down her back. He sped past her place to inspect the trench when his headlights lit up a solid wall of white.

Jordan slammed on the brakes and skidded into the drift that had blocked off the trench. The drift was at least eight feet high, higher in some places. There was no exit. Poking out of the drift were twisted pieces of metal and shards of rock.

Jordan shook as he picked up his radio.

The old bat saw something funny, all right. Fucking hilarious, he thought to himself.

"It was them Tinsel men," a woman's voice said. Jordan spun around and found Minnie standing near his cruiser, wrapped in a down parka and wearing heavy black boots. "The goddamn Tinsel men blew up a snowplow. On purpose!"

"What?"

"You heard me all right. I watched 'em do it. I was right there on my porch. Floyd and his son Randy, they drove a snowplow down over there and blew the thing up. It nearly blew in my windas."

Jordan's hands shook, but he found the transmit button on the radio and pushed it.

"Kelly. Get Sean on the phone. Right now."

"But he said no calls," Kelly replied.

"This is an emergency."

"Really?" she asked. "What happened?"

"Just get Sean on the phone. Now."

"Well, all right then, gosh," Kelly said. "Hold on."

CHAPTER 14

Samantha Tinsel and her mother had decided to watch a movie. It was an old Christmas one that her mother liked, but her mother had only been able to sit still for ten minutes before she began pacing the floor again. When she wasn't pacing, clutching the phone, she spent her time staring out the big picture window that overlooked the backyard, and beyond that, the forest.

"You're missin' it, Mom," Samantha whined.

Samantha was ten and did not want to watch *White Christmas* for the twentieth time, but only to get her Mom to stop worrying. But now she was stuck watching Bing Crosby dance and sing across an impossibly white soundstage by herself. Not impressed.

"I know, Honey," she said. "I just … as soon as I hear from Sean I'll feel better."

"You were just there, Mom. Even if he left right away he's gonna be gone at least an hour, probably two."

And then Samantha heard it, the low whine of a snowmobile. She was on her feet in a second, standing beside her mother. Two snowmobiles broke through the tree line and headed toward their house.

"Oh, thank God," Nancy whispered and crossed herself. "Thank God."

She ran through the house to the kitchen door, threw it open and wrapped her arms around her husband.

"Oh, thank God," she whispered furiously. She kissed him

hard on the mouth and pulled him close to her.

"I was so worried."

"Okay, okay, honey. It's all right now," he said. "Let's go inside."

"And you!" she said to Randy. "Oh, my God. I was so scared."

Randy smiled nervously and moved into his mother's waiting arms. She squeezed him very tight.

"Thank God you're all right."

Floyd closed the door behind them and locked it. Randy was still holding his mother in a loose hug. She stared up at him, smiling.

Nancy turned to her husband and Floyd brought down a marble rolling pin into the middle of her face with a bone-crushing crack. Nancy's face disappeared for a moment in a gush of red. She sagged in Randy's grip but he squeezed her arms tight to her sides and held her up off the floor. Floyd hit her again, two hands on the rolling pin and he was swinging for the fences. The marble connected squarely across Nancy's face. Blood sprayed and teeth rattled across the tile floor like dice. Nancy started to seizure. Her eyes rolled up white, and blood and spit fell from her trembling lips. Randy dropped her and she fell to the kitchen floor without ceremony. She lay there, face down, as a growing pool of blood spread around her head.

At the doorway stood Samantha, speechless. Her father stared at her across the gap of twelve feet. His pale, unshaven face was speckled with blood. His brown eyes were hard and cold.

"Take her," he said.

Randy sprang from where he stood, flying at her with animal speed. Samantha turned and ran. A scream ripped the air. Her thin arms and legs pumped as fast as they could, propelling her in a straight line to an open door, the downstairs bathroom.

She slammed the door behind her but her brother got his foot in the jamb and wedged the door open. She pushed and pushed but her brother was too strong. With one big shove he flung the door inward and she was tossed against the toilet.

He rushed straight for her. She put up her arms to block the blows but the first hit her above the left eye. The next landed square on her jaw and she tasted blood. Her hands flew to her face and then it was over. He grabbed a handful of her hair and slammed her face against the back of the toilet again and again until the girl went limp.

Randy let go of his sister and she slid to the blood-soaked floor. He heard a noise at the door and found his father standing there watching.

"Bring her out here," he said. "We'll do it in the living room."

CHAPTER 15

She stepped into the kitchen expecting wine and roses and the table set with a dinner straight out of one of her *Country Living* magazines. What she found was the table half set, a bottle of wine on the counter and the kitchen a complete fucking disaster. Shaking her head she pulled a wooden spoon out of a saucepan and the pan came with it. She had to laugh. Sean wasn't even home.

Petra found Sean's note and read it leaning against the windowsill.

Turning back to the kitchen she thought about cleaning up, but decided that it could wait. She made her way down the hall to the bathroom where she ran a hot and deep bubble bath.

When the phone rang, Petra was just slipping her foot into the soapy water. She sighed, pulled on her robe and padded back down the hall to the kitchen.

"Hello?"

Petra wedged the cordless phone between her shoulder and her chin and started picking up the kitchen.

"Petra, it's Kelly. I'm sorry to bother you and I swear it's an emergency, but I need to talk to Sean right now."

"Kelly, Sean's not here."

"What?"

Petra carried the bottle of wine to the fridge along with the china butter dish.

"I just got home," she explained. "Sean left me a note that he was going out to Monk's Head Mine to check on Floyd and

Randy."

"They aren't back yet?" Kelly asked.

"I guess not. What's up?"

"Well, my Jordan took a call to Minnie Wilkes's place, out by the trench, and he says it's an emergency. Could you have Sean call me when he gets in?"

Petra reached for the handle of the fridge and stopped dead. The bottle of wine slipped from her fingers and exploded across the tile floor, followed shortly by the butter dish. Her hand holding the telephone dropped to her side.

"Petra? Are you all right? Petra?" Kelly's voice, sounding very far away, called through the phone.

Without taking her eyes from the new police bulletin that decorated the fridge door, Petra hit the END button on the phone and killed the connection. She set the phone down on the counter and pulled the bulletin from the fridge. The little ladybug magnets that held it in place clattered to the floor.

She studied every pixel of the image, found his eyes, dark and hooded, looking right at her. Right into her. She had heard of the Rayford killings in New York City, but now, to come face to face with their killer this way—was it coincidence, an accident? Not likely, not with this one. He had found her.

CHAPTER 16

Jordan almost called Minnie Wilkes a liar to her face. What he did say was that he was going to check out the Tinsel residence, see if he could get some answers. But she was wrong. She had to be. After all, the old bird was pushing ninety, at least. He thought about calling over to the Tinsels' house, but it really wasn't something you could ask over the phone. "Hey, I was just wondering, did you blow up a snowplow and cause a massive rock slide in the trench?" No, it really wouldn't fly.

He radioed Kelly again, but no, she hadn't heard from Sean yet. This was a shitstorm. Sooner rather than later people were going to notice the trench was blocked, and on purpose. Someone, according to Minnie Wilkes the Tinsel boys, blew up a snowplow that formed a natural barricade, trapping everyone in Danaid. They would want answers, they would be angry and scared, and they would panic. Jordan wasn't ready for that. Not by a long shot. That was Sean's job and he was happy to let him handle it.

But this initial contact was his. He slowed as he approached the Tinsel home. What was the plan? Arrest them? Bring them in for questioning? He swore fiercely at Minnie for sending him here. He cursed Sean for being unreachable at a time like this. He did not want this responsibility.

He pulled into the driveway and killed the engine. He was going to play it cool, he told himself. No accusations, no threats.

With a heavy sigh of resignation he hefted himself out of the cruiser and walked to the front door. He took a deep breath, rang the bell and waited. He rang it again and stepped closer to the door, sneaking a peek into the home through the glass inset. Pictures lined the wall: birthdays, summer vacations, parties. He knew he was in some of them. Randy had been one of his best friends since grade school, before he went off to university.

No one came to the door. He rang again and scanned the inside. The house was dark. He walked back to the cruiser and looked up at the darkened windows of the second floor.

Not home?

He circled around the house to the back door that led to the kitchen. He knocked and knocked to no avail. To his right was a high window that looked over the sink. He dragged over a wooden deck chair that was nearly buried in snow and climbed up. Standing on the arms of the deck chair he could just see into the kitchen. He used his flashlight and found the higher cupboards and the counter. Yup, it was the Tinsel family kitchen. Neat, orderly, clean. Everything in its place.

When he saw the blood on the floor it didn't register at first. He stared at it, as if he couldn't comprehend. Then he saw that it was everywhere. It splattered the white cupboards and pooled on the pale brown tile floor. His light found a wide smear of blood on the floor leading into the living room.

"Jesus Christ," he whispered. He dropped down to the stone patio and moved toward the door, his weapon drawn. He took a couple of steps back and readied himself to kick open the door. He took a deep breath. He had never done this before and he was rightfully nervous. It looked so easy in the movies. How hard could it be? His heart hammered. He took two quick steps and kicked out hard with his right foot. The shooting pain immediately ran up his leg as he rebounded off the door. The sound of him kicking the door was explosive, but apparently his kick wasn't. He hopped painfully to the door and tried the handle. It turned easily in his hand. He didn't know if that was a good sign or bad.

He pushed the door open slowly and took a step inside. In one hand he held his pistol up and ready, in the other, the flashlight. He couldn't take his eyes off the blood on the floor. It stood out against the light brown tile like neon. His stomach rolled over as he tried to guess which one of the Tinsel family was the victim. He felt like puking but he held it back. He gritted his teeth, took one step and then another, deeper into the darkness of the house.

CHAPTER 17

Sean leapt from the moving sled and ran for the back door of his house. He slipped inside, slammed the door and peered out through the window. Floodlights lit the yard behind his house for about fifty feet. Beyond that was darkness. His breath fogged the glass and his heart beat so fast it felt like it would slam into the door in front of him.

He scanned the black and white landscape and listened for the whine of another sled. He heard nothing but the wind, and his own wheezing breath.

All the way home his mind had swirled around what had happened at the mine. *What was going on?* What had chased him? Where were the Tinsels? Nothing made sense.

He moved through the ruined kitchen and called to Petra but got no answer. He stepped around the shattered wine bottle and butter dish. He found the phone on the countertop and snatched it up.

Violet Monroe picked up on the third ring.

"Violet, it's Sean."

"Oh hi, Sean, how's the evenin' going?" she asked.

"Listen, pack Kevin up and meet me and Petra at the police station."

"Why? What happened?"

"I'll tell you when I see you. Just pack up Kevin and get him to the station right now."

Violet sounded shaky and scared when she finally told Sean she would leave right now. Sean hit END and searched the house from room to room.

"Petra?" Sean asked. "Are you here? Petra!"

He found her sitting alone in the darkened living room. The police bulletin he'd brought home for Kevin was on her lap. He whispered her name but she didn't look up. She didn't flinch. She seemed lost in thought.

Sean reached out and touched her shoulder, and her head whipped toward him. Her eyes flashed and for a split second he saw something swell and flex behind her eyes. Something burned there, bright and dark all at once. Cold shivered through Sean's belly.

"I called you," he said. "You didn't hear me?"

Her gaze softened and slowly her head swiveled back to facing front.

"We have to go," he said. "Violet's gonna meet us at the station with Kevin."

Petra's expression didn't change. She stared placidly into the darkness, unfazed.

"Petra, I went to the mine and … and something was there. I think whatever it was tried to kill me. I think it might have killed Floyd and Randy Tinsel. I trapped it behind a door, but I don't know how long it will hold. We have to go. Now."

Sean took the police bulletin from her lap.

"I thought I saw him today at the cemetery," Sean said.

Petra leapt from her seat and stepped toward him. Her face was deadly pale, her eyes wide.

"Then he's here? I knew it. It isn't safe."

"Listen to me, baby," Sean said, taking her by the hands, "It's all right. But we have to go. Something is happening and I don't know what it is. Until I figure it out, I want you and Kevin somewhere safe. Safer than this place. So please, help me get going here."

CHAPTER 18

Kelly was fast asleep in the jail cell when Jordan burst through the front door. She jumped out of her makeshift bed and staggered into the main office area.

"What is it?" she asked, her voice thick with sleep.

"Did Sean call in?"

Jordan's face looked like ash. He was shaking.

"What's wrong, sugar?"

"I would have gone to his house but the station was on my way."

"What are you talking about?"

Kelly was fully awake now and getting more worried by the second. Jordan looked scared and that scared her.

"Jordan, honey, talk to me. What happened?"

Jordan snatched up the phone.

"They're gone," he said. "All gone. Just blood and … skin, left on the floor."

"What?"

But Jordan was dialing a phone number. He misdialed twice he shook so badly. On the third try he heard the phone ring on the other end.

"Oh, come on Sean, answer," Jordan whispered. "Answer the goddamn phone. Please."

He thought about the phone ringing in Sean's house, about Sean and Petra and Kevin reduced to oily curls of skin and the phone ringing on and on and he felt ready to puke. Greasy waves of nausea climbed his throat and he swallowed hard and prayed for Sean to answer.

Sean was in the bedroom throwing clothes in a duffel bag when the phone rang. He grabbed the cordless from the bedside table.

"Jordan, slow down, Jesus Christ. Slow down," he said and then listened to his deputy. "Okay, okay, just stay there. We're coming now. Violet and Kevin should be there any minute. Don't go anywhere till you see me."

Bishop stopped dead at the ringing of the phone. He listened until he heard Sean talking somewhere deep within the house and then moved through the living room.

He found her in the kitchen. A seven-inch blade slid from inside his sleeve into his hand.

From the bottom of the stairs he watched Petra drink orange juice from the carton as she leaned against the counter. Until that moment he had seen only pictures, grainy black-and-whites taken from a distance. Until right then he had tried desperately to treat her like any other target. Not anymore. Tight, tanned skin, auburn hair the color of burnt copper. She was beautiful.

She replaced the carton in the fridge. He couldn't move. The blade felt heavy in his hand, his feet rooted to the floor.

For a moment Bishop hoped that Petra would never turn around. He hoped that she would keep her back to him and walk through the back door to the yard.

Then Petra turned. Her scream shattered the silence.

Bishop charged, blade up and ready to strike. Big strides quickly ate up the distance between them. He was four feet away, reaching out for her, when he was tackled from behind and slammed into the wall. His knife spun across the white tile floor. Sean lay flat across him, pinning Bishop to the floor.

"Run! Get out of here!" Sean screamed as Bishop thrashed and kicked beneath him.

Bishop threw his head back and smashed it into Sean's face. Blood squirted from his nose, running down his chin, and Sean's grip slipped. Bishop squirmed loose and scrambled toward the kitchen table where his knife lay under a chair, but Sean wrenched him back. Bishop drove elbow after elbow into Sean's face, but Sean held on, arms and legs wrapped around the intruder.

"Run, Petra! Run!"

But Petra didn't move.

Blood covered Sean's face and his knees buckled.

Finally, Bishop delivered a knee to Sean's chin that knocked him backwards onto the floor spitting blood toward the ceiling. Bishop scooped up his fallen blade and turned as a butcher knife arced out of the air and straight through his throat. Bishop gurgled a cry as he reeled back, clawing at the blade in his neck. Falling backward, he lashed out at Petra with his own blade and slashed her across the belly. Petra whirled away screaming. She fell against the cupboard as bright crimson bled through her t-shirt.

Sean was barely conscious. He crawled to where Petra sat slumped against the cupboard holding her stomach. Blood flowed freely between her fingers and over her thighs.

"Oh Jesus, no," Sean wailed.

He grabbed a dishtowel and pressed it against her wound. Petra's skin looked waxy, sweaty and white. She shivered from loss of blood.

"C'mon, get up," Sean said

"No, I ..." Petra replied, the rest of her words smothered by a mouthful of blood. Sean wiped her mouth with his hand and said, "You have to. You have to get up. C'mon!"

Sean grabbed her under the arms and lifted her to her feet. Her knees wobbled beneath her. Sean picked her up and carried her in his arms. He snagged his car keys from a hook by the door and stepped out into the snow.

Sean slipped her into the passenger side and pulled on her seat belt. He slid in behind the wheel and peeled out onto the street with the lights flashing and the sirens blaring.

Bloody footprints led down the hall to the bathroom where light spilled from the doorway. Bishop leaned over the sink and stared into the mirror. He fingered the handle of the knife, wriggling the tip of the blade that had pierced his throat just above his Adam's apple. Without ceremony he ripped out the blade. A small stream of blood wept from the wound before it sealed. Soon there was no trace of the injury. He rubbed his newly healed throat.

"Bitch."

He dropped the butcher knife into the sink and headed for the door.

Sean's right hand was pressed against her gushing wound. Petra looked drained. "Stay with me, Honey. Stay awake. C'mon, you can do it," Sean whispered. But Petra's eyelids drooped. Her mouth was slack, her skin white. Sean could barely see the road through the drifting snow.

A pair of headlights gained on them, filling up their rearview until the Bronco rammed them, throwing them forward in their seats. Their seatbelts saved them from kissing the windshield. Sean's Jeep skidded to the right, plowed through the snow and twisted sideways before he regained control and stomped on the gas, putting some distance between them. The Bronco accelerated, charging through the snow to slam into them again.

Sean grabbed the wheel with both hands and fought the skid, as Petra hung limply over her shoulder belt, her hair hanging in her face. "Hold on!" Sean screamed as he spun the wheel and tapped the brakes, skidding through a sharp turn onto a narrow lane.

The Bronco's headlights shook back and forth in the rearview, and for a moment there was nothing but snow and the night behind them. Then the headlights were back.

"Son of a bitch!"

Again Sean goosed the engine as he tried to shake the tail. He turned right onto Old Bridge Road and blew right through the red stop light at the foot of the bridge.

Picking up speed as he hit the wooden planks his eyes were glued to the rearview. He never saw the headlights coming straight at him. A sudden blast from a car horn snapped his eyes forward in time to see a pickup truck barreling down on them. The truck slammed on its brakes. Sean did the same, but it was too late. They slid across the wet boards.

The Bronco ran full tilt into the back of Sean's Jeep. Sean cranked the wheel to the left as the Bronco hit them. The Jeep bounced off the pickup truck and crashed through the side of the wooden bridge, tearing through the old wooden barriers as if they were cardboard.

It exploded through the wall and flew through the air, dropping through twelve feet of darkness to crash headlong into the frozen river, punching through the ice in a spray of black water.

Inside the Jeep there was no sound, no movement except for the water that rushed into the cab.

The stream of cold water brought Sean around. Groggily he twisted in his seat and scanned the situation. He was pinned between his seat and the steering wheel, his face was badly cut, and blood stung his eyes. Petra slumped over her shoulder belt, unconscious.

The Jeep sank as Sean shifted in his seat. The ice splintered and cracked all around them and freezing water bubbled to the surface. Water crept up over Sean's knee. They were running out of time.

The roadway inside the covered bridge was blocked by the twisted vehicles, smoking and ticking in the semi-dark. Bishop shook himself, climbed out of the wrecked Bronco and took a look around. The pickup driver was hunched over his steering wheel: dead or alive he wasn't moving. Bishop stepped to the torn section of the wall and looked down to the frozen river. The Jeep rested half in and half out of the water, but its nose sank fast. He could see movement inside the cab. Bishop turned and ran to the end of the bridge.

Sean reached for Petra and shook her shoulder. "Petra. Petra, honey, you need to get up."

He brushed the hair from her face, and splashed water

over her cheeks. She awoke with a start, looking dazed and confused.

"Sean? What?"

"We have to get out of here. Can you move?"

"I … I think so," she replied faintly.

"Roll down your window." Petra did what she was told and soon she had the window all the way down.

"Okay, good. C'mon, let's go."

Petra lifted herself in her seat and squealed.

"What? What?"

"My ankle! Oh God!" she cried.

Sean looked down at her ankle. Her foot was nearly severed, pinned between two pieces of jagged metal.

"I'm caught. I'm caught," she said.

"Okay. Okay. Hold on."

The Jeep sank lower. Petra screamed.

"It's all right," Sean said, touching her cheek. "It's all right." He tried to smile.

He knelt down in the foot well and tried to free her mutilated foot, to pry the metal pieces apart that held her.

"Try to pull your foot out," he said as he held the metal pieces apart as far as he could, his hands bleeding from the effort.

"I can't!" she screamed.

"You've got to! You've got to! Please, I know it hurts but pull. Pull!"

Petra yanked on her trapped foot, screaming as she pulled, but her foot wouldn't budge. Tears streamed down her face. The water rose.

Sean looked for anything he could use to wedge apart the

metal, but found only a handheld ice scraper. He took a deep breath and then dove under the surface.

The Jeep sank faster now. Sean broke to the surface and tossed away the ice scraper. Six inches of space separated the water and the roof.

Sean and Petra were inches apart, they could feel each other's breath. Sean's mind raced; there's got to be a way out. There has to be something he could use.

"Sean. Please," Petra whispered. "Don't leave me."

Sean held her face in his hands and stared into her blue gray eyes that always reminded him of the sea after a storm. "I won't. I'm not going to leave you."

Sean kissed her and dove down into the water. His fingers were shredded by the shards of metal but he didn't care, he could barely feel them anyway. He wrenched her foot mercilessly. He could hear her screams through the water.

Suddenly, the ice beneath the Jeep broke free.

Bishop made it to the end of the bridge. With his pistol drawn, he scrambled down the bank to the river's edge and started out across the ice toward the Jeep.

At twenty feet away, he stopped and aimed at the back of Petra's head. Suddenly she turned, and for a moment they stared at each other. His pistol aimed and ready, his finger held over the trigger.

The Jeep shifted off the ledge and sank quickly through the dark. The black, freezing water rushed into the cab and filled Petra's mouth, smothering her scream. In the next moment she was gone as they disappeared beneath the ice in a spray of water and black bubbles.

Underwater Sean continued to pull on her leg but it wouldn't budge. He held her face in his hands, stared into her eyes. They held hands. Finally, she let him go. He held on as long as he could, his lungs burning from lack of oxygen. There was nothing he could do but slip past her through the window.

Moments later Sean broke to the icy surface and scrambled up onto the ice. Out of breath, spitting up water, he looked up just in time to see Bishop kick him in the face and knock him unconscious.

Bishop dove into the freezing water. He swam easily with powerful strokes deeper and deeper into the dark. A small flashlight guided him to the wreck of Sean's Jeep, resting on the riverbed. He swam until he could maneuver inside. The blade of his knife flashed.

The Jeep was empty.

CHAPTER 19

Danaid's only medical clinic was run out of the large Victorian home of Doctor Ronald Baron, a small elderly man with a full head of silver hair. A bulky gray cardigan, frayed at the cuffs, hung on his narrow frame as he stepped across the floorboards nearly without sound. He entered from the hall into a small room that looked more like a spare bedroom than a recovery room in some anonymous hospital ward.

To his right he found Violet Monroe, Kevin Berlin and Kelly Fike staring up anxiously at him from the long, deep couch that ran along one wall. The good doctor smiled warmly and moved to the cluster of wheezing and softly beeping machines that had been gathered around his patient. He adjusted the lines and cables, read the various readouts and then retreated from the room just as quietly as he had entered.

"When will he wake up?" Kevin asked. Dr. Baron stepped close to the boy. His little fingers clasped his fathers'. The doctor bent at the waist until they were eye to eye. "Your father's very strong," he whispered. "Very strong." Smiling warmly, he stared into the boy's red-rimmed eyes. "Have faith, boy." Kevin nodded and managed a weak smile. Without another word, the doctor slipped silently out into the hall, passing Deputy Jordan Hanson as he came through the entrance hall.

Jordan's wet boots squeaked over the worn green linoleum to Sean's room, whose door hung halfway open. He eased himself inside and winced at the sight of Sean nearly buried under a pile of heating blankets. All that was visible were the tops of his shoulders, his right arm and his head. But that was enough. His face was a giant bruise, purple and black like a storm cloud with eyes and a mouth. The rest of his skin looked pale gray.

Kelly slipped into place beside him, her face red and her eyes bloodshot. Violet sat at the far end of the couch, running her fingers through Kevin's hair as he lay asleep, his head in her lap. She gave Jordan a weak smile and then returned her stare to the middle distance around Sean.

"How's he doing?" he whispered. Kelly nodded toward the hall and Jordan followed her out. After they closed the door behind them, they took a few steps away from the room along the walls covered with old black and white photographs of an early Danaid: the bridge, the cemetery, the mine. Photos Jordan had seen a hundred times throughout his history of ailments and broken bones.

"Oh, Jesus, Jordan, tell me what's going on?" she whined. "What's happening in this town?"

"I don't know yet. How's Sean?"

"Sean's doing fine, apparently," Kelly said. "Doc says he looks a hell of a lot worse than he is. Mild hypothermia."

Kelly hooked a thumb down the darkened hall. "Harry Stemple, you know, from the dairy farm." Jordan nodded. "He's down there nursing one hell of a headache and a few cracked ribs. Doc says he'll be fine in a couple of days. What about the guy driving the Bronco?"

"Gone."

"Gone? Gone where?"

"Who knows? By the time I got there he was gone. I ran the plates. They were stolen off a mini-van in Denver," he said.

"The Bronco will probably end up being stolen too."

"What's going on, Jordan?" Kelly whispered.

Jordan shook his head.

"I don't know," he said. "People are missing. People I've known all my life are doing crazy things. *Crazy.* It doesn't make any sense. What am I supposed to do?"

He was definitely not trained for this. Things were happening too fast. He took a breath and found it wasn't enough. Kelly moved closer to him and slipped her hand into his.

"Something is happening here, Kelly, and I'm scared to death," he whispered. "We have to get out of this town."

Kelly stared into his eyes and asked, "Leave town? How?"

"Why are you leaving?" Kevin asked.

Jordan and Kelly jumped when they saw Violet and Kevin standing in the hall behind them.

"In case, you know, in case Sean needs to go to Braden," Jordan replied. "Someplace a little more high tech."

"Oh, well, Doc Baron says he should be fine," Violet said.

"I know, I just like to plan for the worst."

"Well, let's hope it doesn't get any worse. I don't think I can handle worse," she said. "I'm taking Kevin home. He's going to need his rest."

"I want to stay," Kevin said.

"I know you do, Honey, but you need to get some sleep. Your daddy's gonna be fine. And we'll be back in the morning."

Kevin broke away from Violet and ran back to his father's side. He bent close to his ear and whispered, "I love you, Dad."

"You want me to drive you home?" Jordan asked, as he watched Violet pull on her coat.

"No thank you," she replied. "Looks like you could use some rest yourself."

Jordan nodded, too tired for anything more than that.

Violet touched his cheek and smiled and said that they would be back in the morning. Kelly agreed to go back to the station and sleep there until Jordan came to relieve her in the morning. Jordan watched them pull away from the front door of the clinic and waved as the trio disappeared slowly into the darkness. As soon as they left, Jordan dropped down into the couch. After two minutes of head bobbing, he was asleep.

CHAPTER 20

Jessica Walters raised her head and winced. She had fallen asleep at her desk again, leaving her neck and shoulders feeling like they had rusted in place. She stretched and rolled her head around on her thin neck to work out the kinks and then scanned the last few paragraphs of her essay.

She was nearly done, but when she picked up her pen she felt her eyelids droop and her stomach growl. She needed food. Right now. She slipped into her Winnie the Pooh slippers, left her room and headed for the stairs.

The kitchen was dark, except for the night-light over the stove. And it was there that she found what she was looking for, her mother's freshly baked apple pie. They had had it for dessert but there were still a few pieces left. Jessica grabbed a fork from the utensil drawer and dug in.

As she ate she gazed out into the black and white emptiness of their backyard through the window over the stove. Snow blew in ragged funnels and white clouds, and for a moment she didn't realize what she was looking at. She set her fork down and stared. Out in the backyard, just beyond the reach of the floodlights, stood—someone. A woman? Jessica couldn't tell. But someone was out there.

Jessica spun away from the window and ran upstairs.

Her parents' room was dark, but she found her father's shoulder and shook it. "Daddy! Daddy!" she whispered. But it was Jessica's mother, Ruth, who woke up. She snapped on the bedside lamp, a worried look already pinching her features.

"What's wrong, Jess?"

"There's a woman outside," she replied.

"Go back to bed, honey," Billy mumbled through his pillow. "Just a dream."

"What woman?" asked Ruth.

Jessica shook her head. "I don't know. She's just standing there."

Ruth shook Billy awake, rolling him over onto his back.

"What?" he hissed, wincing as the lamplight stabbed at his eyes. "What woman?"

"Go check," Ruth said. "Please?"

Billy rubbed the sleep out of his eyes, trying to get his wife to come into focus. "Are you serious?" He could tell by her look that she was, and with a heavy sigh he swung his legs out from under the covers and turned to his daughter.

"Show me."

A minute later, Jessica, Billy and Ruth were huddled against the window over the stove, peering out into the backyard. It was a woman all right, wearing a red t-shirt by the looks of it, dark hair plastered to her scalp, thin and white, looking like she was frozen solid standing out there in the cold.

"Call Sean," Ruth said nervously. "I don't like this."

Billy shuffled to the back door and pulled his coat down off its peg.

"Where're you going?" asked Ruth.

"Out to see," Billy replied. "She could be hurt."

Ruth peered through the window again at the woman standing motionless in the snow. "Looks stoned, or crazy. Or both."

Billy pulled on his toque and his gloves and stepped out into the storm.

From the kitchen window Ruth watched her husband strip off his coat and wrap it around the woman.

"Jess, give me the phone."

"Who're you callin'?"

"Never mind. Just give me the phone."

Jessica pulled the cordless phone from the cradle mounted on the wall and handed it to her mother as she watched her father guide the woman back through the blowing snow to the house.

"Ruth! Ruth!"

Ruth appeared at the back door, one hand holding her robe closed at her throat, the other holding the phone to her ear.

"Jesus Christ, is that Petra?" she said as she stared at the woman her husband held tight.

Billy nodded frantically. "Call Sean. Get him over here."

"I am," she replied. "There's no answer."

"We gotta get her out of these clothes."

"There's clean ones in the laundry room," Ruth said. "C'mon, honey." Ruth took Petra by the shoulders and led her through the kitchen to the small laundry room. Jessica watched as her mother baby-stepped Petra behind the door. Ruth caught Jessica's eye as the door closed and gave her daughter a little "it'll be all right" wink and a smile.

Billy dialed again, as he squeezed the phone in his huge fist. He looked scared and nervous. He was wide awake now, that was for sure.

"What can I do, Dad?"

Billy hung up and leaned against the counter with his arms crossed.

"Umm, could you run a bath for her, honey?" asked Billy. "Not too hot, okay. She'll be up in a minute."

"Okay."

Jessica took the stairs two at a time. Soon, Billy heard the water pipes rattle and shake as Jessica filled the tub. Billy dialed Sean again and listened to the phone ring. Finally, after the tenth ring he stabbed the disconnect button and started opening drawers and looking into cabinets.

Piles of neatly folded laundry were arranged on a small card table. Ruth found a pair of jeans, a bulky woolen sweater and some underwear. She held up a pair of her jeans to Petra's narrow waist and said, "You're gonna need a belt, honey." She tried to smile, but Petra's eyes never flickered. Ruth's smile died on her lips.

"C'mon, let's get you out of these clothes."

Ruth rolled up the stained t-shirt and slipped it over Petra's head. She then circled to the front and rolled it down over her arms. Petra never moved. Standing there alone with Petra in the small narrow laundry room made Ruth more than a little uncomfortable, and not just because she was naked. Petra's lips were parted, her blue-gray eyes stared vacantly ahead, but her chest didn't move. It was quiet in the laundry room, the only sound the distant rattle of the water pipes and Billy rummaging around in the next room. Ruth stepped closer to Petra and listened. She had her ear nearly pressed to Petra's cold lips.

Petra wasn't breathing.

"Where's the goddamn phonebook?" Billy yelled through the door. "Ruth? Ruth?"

Ruth jumped and made a wide circle around Petra to the laundry room door where she peered out.

Billy stepped to the crack and whispered, "I need the phonebook, I'm gonna call Doc Baron. Where is it?"

"It's in the hall, in the china cabinet."

"Well, why would it be there?"

"'Cause that's where it is," Ruth said, and slammed the door.

Petra hadn't moved, but something was different. Ruth tiptoed closer, studying her. Something was wrong. Petra was trembling. Her entire body shivered.

"Oh, God," Ruth whispered. Petra wasn't shivering, wasn't trembling. Her skin was moving. On its own. Her pale gray skin darkened as swirls and symbols of black rose to the surface. It began at her fingertips.

"Billy," Ruth whispered.

The strange markings swept up over Petra's hands, reaching up her arms.

"Billy."

Black tendrils swept over her arms and chest, broke across her face and pooled in her blue-gray eyes, smothering their color with black. For one breathless moment, Ruth saw the rest of her life in Petra's obsidian eyes.

And for the first time, Petra looked at Ruth and smiled. It was then that Ruth began to scream.

CHAPTER 21

Bishop stood under the showerhead for a very long time, letting the hot water run over his neck and down his back. His hands were pressed to the tile wall, his eyes closed. Behind his eyes the past and present were cut together to play in a vengeful loop in his head: his wife asleep in the sun, her skin warm, the color of caramel; Petra standing in the kitchen, her long, thin legs sliding up into the hem of her t-shirt.

She turned.

Her eyes, drowsy from the sun, slowly rolled open. Her cheek, her profile, the side of her eye. He was helpless as he watched. He saw himself reflected in her empty, black eyes. But not him. What he had become.

He opened his eyes. The water had run cold. He twisted the taps closed and stepped out of the shower. He found clean clothes folded on the lid of the toilet. He dressed quickly and passed over the creaking floorboards down the hall to his room.

Norman stood staring out the window, his back to Bishop as he entered.

"This thing, it ain't over, is it?" Norman asked.

Norman waited for a reply as he continued to watch the white fields shift left, then right, carried on the swirling wind.

"I can finish this," Bishop said.

"There are good people here."

"I can finish this, Norman."

Norman turned to face him. "I hope so," he replied. "'Cause

it's not gonna get any easier." Norman nodded toward the darkening window. "Storm's brewing."

⚜

Jordan awoke to the sound of drawers being opened and closed, shuffling feet and a whispered voice pleading, "Please, Mr. Berlin. Please, you must get back to bed." Jordan shielded his eyes against the sunlight that streamed into the recovery room and sat up. Sean spotted him.

"Good, you're awake. Help me find my clothes."

Jordan rubbed sleep from his eyes, not completely awake.

Sean turned to Dr. Baron who followed him around the room closing drawers Sean left open. "I need to borrow some clothes," Sean said.

"I'm afraid that's out of the ordinary. I don't think—"

"Now," Sean said. "Right now."

The Doc took one look at Sean and decided to keep his mouth shut. He turned on his heel, muttering something that sounded like, "I'll see what I can do," and disappeared out into the hall.

"What are you doing up?" Jordan got to his feet, wincing as he stretched the kinks in his back.

"I gotta get out of here," Sean said. "I can't do anything lying in bed."

"But the doc says—"

"Listen, I'm leaving. You can come along and help me or go home. It's up to you."

The front receptionist Jordan had seen the night before came quietly into the room with a pile of clothes—sweatpants, t-shirt, a raincoat and a pair of old sneakers. Sean took them and put them on.

Less than ten minutes later he stepped slowly through his kitchen. The place looked like a slaughterhouse. Blood splattered across the natural wood cabinets and pooled on the tiled floor. He had seen the same scene a hundred times before—the blood, the signs of a struggle—but he never thought that the house he would find this in would be his own. Jordan didn't say a word.

"I saw him die, Jordan," Sean whispered as he crouched low to the ground next to the largest of the blood puddles. "Right here. I saw him die. I was trying to hold him, you know, away from Petra, but he twisted away and then he screamed. Petra stabbed him in the throat." Sean absently rubbed his own throat as he remembered the way that the handle protruding from Bishop's throat glistened, slick with blood. The way it slipped through the man's fingers. Sean followed the bloody footprints up the stairs and said, "No one could get up from that. No one."

He followed the trail of blood to the bathroom where he found the butcher knife lying in the sink. Jordan stood over his shoulder staring at the blood-splattered porcelain.

"How could he walk away from that?" he asked. "Jesus."

"I'm going to pack some things," Sean said. "For Kevin and me. I'll meet you back in the truck." Jordan nodded and retreated down the hall toward the kitchen.

After Jordan was gone, Sean stepped down into the bedroom and stripped off the borrowed clothes. He started to dress, not realizing how many pictures of him and Petra and Kevin were scattered throughout the bedroom. He tried not to look, reaching for his sock drawer, but found himself staring into Petra's eyes. The picture had been taken in the summer, down by the lake. The sun was on her face. God, she was beautiful. Sean closed his eyes. She begged him, her voice trembling, "Please, Sean, please don't leave me."

Hot tears burned down over his cheeks. He tried to control it, keep it at bay, but the pain and misery that twisted inside him rushed up from his stomach like a wave. He smelled her in the sheets of the unmade bed. Her clothes lay scattered across the floor. Soon his shoulders shook. He sat in the darkened bedroom, on the edge of the bed, holding Petra's picture, and wept.

Jordan was halfway through his third cigarette when Sean stepped from the house. He stubbed out the butt in the ashtray and turned down the radio.

"Move over," Sean said.

Jordan turned to find Sean standing at the driver's side door. His eyes were red and his look gave Jordan no option. Without a word the deputy climbed into the passenger seat as Sean slid behind the wheel.

"Where we going?" asked Jordan.

Sean drove a little too fast for Jordan's liking, fishtailing around corners, sliding through stop signs, but they got there in record time, especially in the snow. They finally parked in the northwest corner of the Danaid Cemetery and stepped out into the snow.

"What are we doing here, Sean?"

Jordan pulled another cigarette to his lips and waited for an answer. Sean didn't give one. He stepped one way, down a few rows, and then came back, looking for something.

"It looks different from in here," he said.

Sean finally seemed to catch the scent of the thing he was after and took off marching through the lines of plots toward the fence. Jordan followed.

When Sean started to run, Jordan lost sight of him for a second. Suddenly he found himself alone among the tombstones. He turned in a circle, scanning the cemetery, and spotted Sean next to two tall, thin grave markers. When he was close enough, he realized that there were actually three tombstones, two tall ones bracketing a smaller third. He read the inscriptions:

Bishop Kane
1940 – 1976

Sara Elizabeth Kane
1941 – 1976

Eve-Marie Kane
1966 – 1976

"He was here," Sean whispered.

Jordan looked at the gravestones, each in turn, and then back at his boss.

"Who?"

"The guy from last night. The same guy stood right here looking at these gravestones," Sean said. "I saw him and he looked right through me."

Jordan watched his boss, waiting for him to make the connection.

"Who are these people?" Jordan asked. "Why would he visit

these graves? They his parents?"

They looked at each other and said, "Norman."

CHAPTER 22

The deadbolt slid back and the door creaked open. Norman peered out at them from between the door and the frame. "What's going on, Sheriff?"

Sean's face was swollen and bruised, but his eyes burned with the ferocity of a zealot.

"I need your help, Norman," Sean said. "Can we come in?" Sean wasn't asking. He stepped over the threshold before Norman could answer.

Norman threw a nervous look over his shoulder.

"Jesus Christ, what happened to your face?" Norman asked as he stepped aside, allowing the two men inside.

"Have you seen any suspicious people in the area?" asked Sean. "Or had any out-of-town visitors lately?"

"Visitors?" Norman replied, shaking his head. "No, can't say as I have. You guys looking for somebody?"

"Norman," Sean said. "Petra's dead."

"Dead?" he whispered. "How? When?"

"Last night a man broke into our house and tried to kill her. We got away but he followed us and ran us off the Old Bridge. Petra drowned. I saw the man who did it. Here."

"Here?" Norman asked, his eyes looking anywhere but at Sean. "Jesus, Sean. My God."

"Yesterday. He was standing at one of the plots out there in the northwest corner. I need to know what he was doing out there in the cemetery."

Norman nodded, yes, yes.

"But folks that come here to pay their respects don't usually check in with me, you know," Norman said. "It's a free country, and everything."

Jordan moved toward the stairway that led upstairs. "Mind if I have a look around?" he said as he started up the stairs.

Norman nodded, but he didn't take his eyes off Jordan climbing the stairs.

"You all right, Norman?" Sean asked.

"Yeah, sure, just a little shaken up is all. I mean, I can't believe it. I just, jeez … I'm sorry, Sean."

"Open your web site," Sean ordered. He stood behind Norman as he sat down at his computer, clicked on the web site and called up the search engine. Norman dragged the cursor to a waiting box.

"What was the name?"

As Sean spoke their names, Norman's hands slipped away from the keyboard to his lap. The old man's shoulders slumped forward as he tried to turn in his seat.

"Sean," was all he could get out before the barrel of Sean's pistol pressed at the base of his head.

"Do it." Norman's fingers stayed where they were. "Now."

Norman found the keyboard and typed in the request. As the message SEARCHING scrolled across the screen, Norman whispered, "Please Sean, take Kevin and go."

The computer chimed and announced that it had found one related article. Sean poked Norman with the gun barrel and Norman clicked on the link to the article.

It was a short obituary of Bishop, Sara and Eve-Marie Kane. The family was killed when a gas leak triggered an explosion, obliterating their house. Norman scrolled to the bottom of the article where a small black and white picture showed the Kane family.

The barrel dropped from Norman's head and nearly dropped from Sean's hand. He stared at the computer screen, at the smiling family. It was too much to be a resemblance. Too close to be a coincidence. It was him. Bishop Kane.

Norman's head fell forward, his eyes turned away from the computer screen. "Please, Sean. Take Kevin away from here. Leave this place before you lose anything else."

Sean stared down at the scared old man looking up at him, pleading with him.

"Please. Leave."

Jordan stepped into what looked like a spare bedroom. Single bed, narrow chest of drawers, a lamp on the chest and a picture of a seascape on the wall. Strictly for the odd guest, he thought. He opened the drawers and then checked under the bed. "Well, what do we have here?"

He pulled out the battered, black leather suitcase and dropped it onto the bed. He released the clasps and the case opened with a creak. Rows of knives and other edged weapons, carefully stacked clips of ammunition and explosives were neatly packed in the worn case. He whistled through his teeth and whispered, "Goddamn."

He left the case open, turned toward the closet and bumped into a pale man in a leather coat. Jordan's eyes popped open and he reached for his gun. The man drove his right fist into the deputy's solar plexus driving him to his knees. Jordan fought to pull his gun, but the man slapped his hand away and squeezed the boy's throat, getting his full attention.

"You don't understand. You probably never will. If you want to live, tell him. Tell him to take his son and leave this place. Now." Jordan struggled for air as the man squeezed his windpipe then let him drop to the floor.

Sean looked up at the ceiling at the sound of a weight hitting the floor above. "Jordan!"

Sean bounded up the stairs and reached the bedroom as the tail of Bishop's leather coat slipped through the window and disappeared. Sean ran to the open window but Bishop was gone. Behind him Jordan struggled to his knees, sucking wind, rubbing his throat and his chest.

"Are you all right?" Sean asked as he bolted past him to the door.

He ran down the stairs, through the kitchen and exploded through the side door out into the cold. Norman's pickup was backing out of the drive as Sean ran after it. He aimed for the windshield and put a bullet six inches from center. The pickup's tires spun over the ice and snow, and for a moment Sean gained on it. He aimed low and hit the hood. The pickup finally grabbed enough road to blast forward, jerking left and right down the narrow lane. Sean reached the lane, out of breath and shaking from the adrenaline, and fired twice at the fading taillights before they turned right onto Quaker Road and disappeared.

Sean came back into the house and found Norman and Jordan in the kitchen. Norman sat slumped in a kitchen chair. The gray skin of his face hung loosely from his skull. He looked about a thousand years old.

"You don't understand," he said.

Sean ripped the old man out of his seat like he was a bundle of rags and slammed him against the wall, rattling dishes and knocking a calendar to the floor. Jordan moved to get between them but froze when Sean drew his gun.

Ruby snapped to attention with a low growl in her throat.

"I don't understand? Is that what you said? I don't understand?" Sean asked, pushing the barrel of his gun to Norman's cheek. "I understand that my wife is dead. Dead, you fuck!"

"Sean," Norman pleaded.

"Who is he? What does he want? Why did he kill Petra? What the fuck is going on here?"

Norman slumped in Sean's grip, but Sean pulled him up straight.

"Sean, please, I don't—"

Sean slammed him against the wall again. The man's ribcage creaked under the pressure. Norman's bony hands, like bird's claws, tried to pry his hands away.

"You fucking know. You know. Who is he? I saw him take a knife in the throat and keep coming. What is he? Bishop Kane. He died over thirty years ago. He's buried out there in the cemetery. Now tell me what you know!"

Finally, Norman began to sob. "You have to leave. Please. You have to go. Right now. Take Kevin."

Sean pulled Norman's face up close to his own.

"Don't you ever say his name again."

"If you don't leave," he whispered, "she'll come for him."

"Who? Who will come for him?"

"Petra," he croaked. "She'll come for all of us."

Sean stared into the old man's wild eyes and shook his

head.

"Jesus Christ," he whispered. "Get your coat." He let go of Norman letting him sink to the floor.

Petra … will come for him.

CHAPTER 23

It was twenty after eight and the sun was having a hell of a time trying to break through the snow clouds that hung low to the town when Kelly drove past the Trading Post.

Gertie sat on a bench, bundled from head to toe in homemade gear: knitted hat, scarf, even her coat was a heavy cable knit job with big round wooden buttons. The only thing store-bought was her Thinsulate gloves, the ones where she could button back the mitten part to uncover her fingers, just in case she was outside doing something that required finger dexterity. Like chain-smoking her way through a fresh pack of Marlboros.

Kelly pulled the Jeep over close to the covered porch of the store and rolled down her window.

"Closed today, Gertie?"

Gertie shrugged her bony shoulders and lit a new smoke with the old one before she pitched the old one into the snow. "Not that I know of. All I know is that I'm freezing my baggy ass off."

"Hop in."

Gertie slid inside and put her thin fingers to the air vent and moaned as the heat warmed her papery skin.

"Where's Billy?"

"Don't know," Gertie replied. "Called his house but there's no answer. I was gonna head over to Mabel's and wait him out."

Kelly's stomach dropped. She buried her face in her hands.

"Jesus, Kelly, what's wrong with you? You gonna be sick?"

Kelly shook her head. After a moment she straightened up and took a deep breath.

"You knocked up? Got morning sickness?" Gertie asked.

"No," she hissed. "God no. Just, I don't know, flu, I guess."

Kelly knew what was coming next and silently begged her not to ask. Please ask me to drive you anywhere in the state but over to the Walters' house. Please God, if you're listening, please don't let her ask me.

"You think you could run me up to Billy's house to see what's what?"

When Sean and Jordan arrived at the station, it was deserted. Kelly wasn't due in for another ten minutes. Jordan led Norman to their only cell and pushed him inside. Norman sat on the end of the cot with a squeak of rusted springs.

"Please Sean, listen to me. Please!"

"Tell me what you know," Sean said. "Who am I chasing?"

Norman's eyes were red-rimmed and ringed with black.

"Tell me!" Sean thundered. "Who am I chasing? Who did this? The guy at your house—"

"He's here to save us, Sean."

"By killing Petra?"

"Yes. "

Sean gripped the bars and lowered his head.

"There was no other way. She had to be destroyed."

Norman reached through the bars and touched Sean's hand.

"I know it's hard to accept—"

Sean grabbed Norman through the bars. He pulled the old

man off his cot and slammed his face into the metal cage. Blood gushed from his head where the bars dug in.

"You listen to me, you crazy fuck," Sean spat, "I don't know what happened to you, old age, mental breakdown, I don't give a fuck. You and your little friend who ran away from us are never leaving this town. I swear to God. I'm gonna bury you here for what you did to Petra and the others."

Sean slammed Norman against the bars again, bringing fresh blood.

"You hear me?" he repeated, whispering fiercely. "I'm gonna bury you."

Sean let Norman go and he folded to the floor, lying in a crumpled pile against the bars.

"Take your son and leave while you can," Norman whispered.

Sean turned back to him.

Norman spat a mouthful of blood. Letting his gaze drift from Sean to Jordan, he said, "They're everywhere now. All around you. And they will take you."

Kelly dropped the Jeep into gear and muttered, "Sure." She wiped cold sweat from her forehead as she checked her mirrors and pulled out into the lane heading north to the Walters' house.

They found the house dark, quiet. Standing at the front door they heard no sound inside. No radio, no conversation. It felt empty. She knocked again.

Gertie stomped her feet and hugged herself, a constant tendril of smoke rising past her pale blue toque.

"Billy? Ruth? Open up!" Gertie yelled. "It's cold out here,

dammit."

After a moment of staring at the empty windows, Kelly suggested that they try the back door, and with a puff of smoke from Gertie's Marlboro, they disappeared around the corner of the house.

They passed the windows of the attached garage and peered inside. Both vehicles were there, a black Dodge Durango and a green mini-van with The Trading Post emblazoned in orange on the side. Kelly and Gertie continued on to the back of the house and as they rounded the corner they stopped dead in their tracks.

The back door hung open, bumping against the frame. Neither spoke. Something was definitely wrong. It was cold outside, no doubt about that, but a whole new kind of cold filled their insides.

"I don't like this," Gertie said. She scanned the backyard as they listened to the door swing, gently creaking on its hinges.

"Stay out here," Kelly said.

Gertie threw another nervous glance around the darkening yard. "Out here? Alone?" she asked. "Why?"

"Just because. I'm the deputy," Kelly replied. "I have to go in. You don't. Go back to the Jeep and lock the doors."

"You're scaring me, Kelly. I can't go back to the Jeep alone."

"Why?"

"Someone could be waiting for us to split up."

"Who?"

"I don't know."

Kelly shook her head.

"Okay," Kelly said. "Just stay behind me, okay? Right behind me."

Gertie nodded and followed the back of Kelly's government issue brown parka through the swinging back door.

"You have no idea what she is, Sean," Norman pleaded. "No idea. The Ministry of the Wraith has been trying to find her for a decade. She's a virus. An infection. She moves from town to town, place to place, and spreads her disease."

"Don't you fucking talk about her," Sean snapped.

"You have to understand. She is a door. A door to—"

"Where? A door to where?"

"Another place."

Sean snorted and fell back into his chair.

"Another place?" he said, "That's the best you can come up with?"

"I don't know where they come from. There's a world beneath the one you know, a world you can't even see," Norman said, almost in a whisper. "But they see you. Through the doors. And they wait and wait for one door to open. Just one. And then they come."

Snow had blown into the house across the mudroom floor, dusting the coats and hats that hung on a pegboard. Gertie closed the door and Kelly jumped.

"What?" Gertie asked. "What?"

"Don't touch anything. Nothing. Okay?"

"Okay," Gertie said, her hands held up in front of her.

The kitchen smelled of apple pie. On the stove the pie plate, with a fork left in it, sat on a burner. Everything else looked untouched.

The snow melted from Kelly's hair and ran over her cheeks and down the nape of her neck.

"Billy? Ruth?" she called out. "It's Kelly."

"And Gertie," added Gertie.

Kelly headed toward the hall. Gertie whispered her name. Kelly turned and found Gertie frozen in place. She followed Gertie's gaze to a door off the kitchen left half open. A thin stream of blood ran from beneath the door out over the cream tile floor.

Blindly, Kelly's fingers fumbled with the strap that held her pistol securely in her holster. She had never drawn her weapon on duty, and only once on the firing range out near Monk's Head Mine after Jordan had told her that she should at least practice, "'cause you never now, right?" She drew the weapon and was surprised at how heavy it was. Her stomach lurched like it always did when she stood at the edge of someplace way too high for her liking. As she made her way slowly to the door, she aimed her pistol at the gap between the door and the frame.

With her left hand she eased open the door.

"Stay out in the kitchen," she whispered.

"What is it?" Gertie asked, edging toward the door.

"Just stay out there."

Blood had splashed across the washer and dryer, small red dots even found their way onto the piles of folded laundry nearby. Blood had pooled on the floor, and handprints were printed in red across the tile. There was blood, a lot of it, but no body. Kelly swept her pistol over the small room, aiming at the shadowed places around the crowded appliances, but there was nothing. She backed out of the room just the same, her pistol trained on the empty space.

"What was it?" Gertie asked from a safe distance away. Kelly didn't answer, her mouth was as dry as if she'd been chewing chalk. Her heart pounded.

They're dead.

They're dead, was all she could think. Somewhere in the house she would find them all. Dead. Oh, Jesus God.

She hadn't prayed since she was a little girl in Sunday school when Father Marin, a wide, short man with a full dark beard smelling of the peppermints he always had in his mouth, would kneel beside her and lead her through, but she remembered just the same.

"Our Father," she whispered, "who art in Heaven."

With the kitchen behind her, Kelly walked past the stairs toward the living room in a trance. She stepped down the hall, the hardwood creaking under her weight. With her mind swimming in adrenaline, every creak sounded like cracking ice. The weight of the pistol in her hand made her shoulder ache, as her gun arm pointed straight down the hall to the living room doorway.

"Hallowed be thy name. Thy kingdom come …"

She shuffled past the main floor bathroom without a sideways glance, for she knew where they were now. Her eyes were locked onto the shreds of blue carpet attached to the floor just inside the door. The walls were bare. No pictures, no lamps or plants. Everything was gone.

"Thy will be done …"

She stepped to the threshold and stopped. Her whispered prayer died on her lips. Every chair, every end table, every stick of furniture had been pushed, thrown, and piled at the far end of the room, nearly blocking the floor-to-ceiling windows entirely from view. The royal blue carpet lay crumpled in a twisted heap, exposing the bare floorboards.

Kelly lowered the gun to her side, letting the heavy lump of metal dangle from her hand.

Except for the furniture, the room was empty.

From where she stood she could see every corner. Unless they were buried under the pile of furniture, Billy, Ruth and Jessica weren't here.

She took a step onto the bare flooring and felt the dirt and grit grind under her boot. Her slow, scraping footfalls echoed hollowly around the room. She took another step and then another, staring down at the center of the floor.

Sean shook his head, too angry and confused to speak. Jordan edged closer.

"What's this Ministry of the Wraith?" Jordan asked.

"It's an organization to protect us," Norman answered.

"Protect us from what?"

"From the evil."

"Petra wasn't evil," Sean shouted. "I knew her better than anyone and I loved her. Everyone in this town did."

"A hunter was dispatched to kill her before she could bring any others through the door," Norman went on quietly.

"From the other place."

"Yes."

Sean raised a cup of coffee toward Norman's cell, "Congratulations then, on a job well done."

Norman shook his head as he stared into his lap.

"It's not over," Norman said. "The hunter failed."

"Petra is dead," Sean whispered. "It's over."

"She's not dead, Sean. The door is open. It's already begun. If the hunter fails, we will all awaken. We will all become."

"Become what?"

"They're called Zijin," Norman answered. "And they're vicious. They can move among us and look just like you or me, but when they hunt, they—"

Somewhere in the background, a phone rang. Jordan picked it up on the first ring.

"Kelly? Where are you?" he asked. "What are you doing there?"

Sean stared hard at Norman. Norman stared back. Nothing the old man said made any sense. There was no Ministry of the Wraith, no Zijin, and whoever or whatever this guy was, he was no supernatural hunter. He was a man, plain and simple. A man who could take a butcher's knife in the throat and keep on coming. He pushed the thought away.

Sean looked to Jordan who was rising fast out of his seat, his face pale. His hand shook as he tried to clip his radio to his belt.

"Sean," Jordan whispered.

Jordan's face was the colour of ash.

"What is it?" Sean asked.

"Kelly's at the Walters' place."

"And?"

"It's bad," was all he could say.

CHAPTER 24

When Sean and Jordan pulled up to the Walters' home, they found Kelly and Gertie sitting in Kelly's Jeep. Gertie had the window rolled down a quarter of the way. A small pile of cigarette butts lay in the snow as she chain-smoked, taking quick drags, her fingers shaking as she tapped the ashes out the open window.

When Kelly got out of the truck, Gertie didn't budge. She sat where she was and didn't speak. She looked green and shriveled, buried under all her winter gear. Kelly ran to Jordan and threw her arms around him.

"What is it?" Sean asked, pulling his collar up against the wind. "Are they in there?"

Kelly was crying, her head buried in Jordan's shoulder, her back shaking. Her gloved hands gripped Jordan tight.

Sean waited. He remembered happier times when he, Petra and Kevin would come here for barbeques in the summer, hockey games in the winter. The house never looked like this. This cold. This gutted.

Kelly lifted her face from Jordan's parka and wiped her red eyes with the back of her hand.

"There's something on the floor in the living room," Kelly said. "I don't know what it is. It looks like people."

Sean asked a few more questions and Kelly answered them as best she could until she started to cry again. They left her outside.

Stepping through the kitchen they saw the blood in the laundry room and kept moving toward the living room.

In the center of the floor three human figures were drawn in blood. Each figure was composed of symbols and characters drawn expertly into a tapestry of red. Sean crouched low enough to inspect the drawing of a human hand. He followed tiny grooves scratched in the wood. A woman's long tapered fingernail stuck up from a floorboard. A shiver ran down his back as he tried to imagine what manner of horror had fallen upon this family. He thought of Ruth and Billy and little Jessica. She was only fourteen.

"What are they?" Jordan asked, getting close to the floor, staring hard at the mysterious shapes. Sean shook his head. He had no answers.

A few minutes later when Sean and Jordan emerged from the house, Sean felt oddly detached. He found himself wondering how normal everyday things could continue after what they had seen. The world waited for no one, you either kept running or you got plowed under.

Kelly and Gertie hadn't moved. The pile of cigarettes outside Gertie's door hadn't grown either. She must be out. She had her arms wrapped around herself, her head down. Kelly stepped out into the cold.

"I'll take Gertie home," she said.

"No, it's all right," Sean replied. "I'll take her. You two head back to the station."

They didn't complain. Jordan wrapped an arm around Kelly and led her to Sean's Jeep. Sean even thought he saw a flicker of a smile on Kelly's lips.

CHAPTER 25

Hours after dropping Gertie at her house, Sean climbed the stairs, opened the door to Violet's kitchen and walked right into her glare. She leaned against the counter, her arms crossed over her heavy breasts.

"Where the hell have you been?" she began.

"Violet—"

"You didn't see his face when we went back this morning, and you were gone, without so much as a phone call. Then you disappear for the whole day. What were you thinking?"

"Violet, look, I'm sorry. There's so much happening, so much I don't understand. I'm just tring to figure it out. It doesn't make any sense. None of it."

"I'll tell you what don't make sense. Keeping your son in the dark. That don't make no sense at all. Keepin' him guessin'. Keepin' us all guessin'. I called the station and Kelly and Jordan don't know where you're at. We're all thinking the worst. Thinking you're gone too."

"I'm sorry, Violet. I've just got figure out what to do. It's bad out there."

"Don't be sorry to me. I know what you're tryin' to do. But he needs you. He needs you now, Sean."

She spun away and started peeling a potato.

"Go talk to you son."

"Where is he?"

Without turning around, Violet pointed down the hall wit her potato peeler.

Sean eased open the bedroom door. The light from the hall fell on his son's face. He was in his pajamas, sitting up in bed, waiting for his dad. His blue eyes opened wide and his mouth pulled into a smile when Sean slipped through the door. Looking at his son, Sean saw his wife smiling back at him and he felt a pain in his chest that stole his breath away.

"Hi."

"You all right?"

Kevin nodded and Sean slipped around the door into the room. He took a seat on the edge of the bed and sat there patiently. He wanted to say something, but nothing came. Kevin stared at him.

Finally, Kevin asked, "Dad?"

"Yeah?"

"Are you going to catch the man that killed Petra?"

Instantly Sean felt the rage that had run through him at the station. He bit back the urge to say, "Yes, of course I'm going to catch him, tie him to a fucking tree and make him beg me to let him die."

"Are you, dad?" Kevin repeated.

"I'll find him," Sean replied. "I promise."

Kevin looked relieved. His tiny shoulders relaxed and his smile grew because at that age a boy believes in the strength of promises.

Sean leaned in close and kissed his son on his forehead. "Now, get some sleep."

Kevin threw his arms around his dad's neck and held him tight. In his arms Kevin felt so small, so vulnerable. Sean squeezed him harder.

"I love you, Dad."

"I love you too, Kev," Sean whispered.

"Could you stay with me?" Kevin asked. "Just till I fall asleep?"

"Sure."

Kevin made room on the double bed and Sean slipped in beside him. Kevin curled up close to his father, a hint of a smile on his face for the first time in a long time. Sean held his son close, felt the warmth of his body, the delicate beat of his heart.

"I miss her," Kevin whispered, his face buried in Sean's chest.

"I miss her too," Sean said. "Go to sleep."

Kevin squeezed his father tight and closed his eyes.

Kelly washed her face with soap and water and tied her hair back into a ponytail. Nothing was going to take down the swelling of crying all day, but at least the smear of eyeliner and mascara were gone. With her face freshly scrubbed a bright pink, she snapped off the bathroom light and stepped out into the main office.

Since she had been gone, Jordan had fallen asleep in his chair, his head hanging off the back leaving his wide neck exposed. His Adam's apple bobbed as he snored.

She shook him gently. "Honey, wake up."

Jordan awoke with a start, snorting as his eyes popped wide. He looked around the station house as if he'd never been there.

"Go home," Kelly said.

"No, it's okay," he replied, his voice thick with sleep. "I'm okay."

"You're tired, honey, look at you."

Jordan leaned over his knees and rubbed his face.

"Jeez."

"Yeah, go home, catch a few winks. Then come on back in a couple hours and relieve me, okay?"

He nodded and pulled himself to his feet.

"Give me a kiss," she said, tapping her puckered lips. Jordan obliged with a quick peck and then she walked him to the door.

"I'll be back soon," he said.

"Drive safe."

Jordan opened the door and winced as the cold wind ripped into him.

"I'll see you soon," he said then disappeared into the storm.

Bishop drove in circles, staying away from the downtown area until he found a dark spot behind a few shops off the main street.

The situation was quickly spinning out of control. He had let the target go. She had escaped. He needed to find her. Bishop slammed his fist against the steering wheel. He took a deep breath, one in, one out, and tried to calm down. This wasn't over.

Inside the cab the temperature dropped sharply. His slow deep breaths shrouded him in mist.

"Where is she, Oliver?"

"We're looking," Oliver replied. "But it's getting worse out there. Reports are coming in from all over town."

Oliver explained that the Zijin were sweeping through the

little Alaskan town like wildfire. Of the hundred and seventy-three people left in the town, the wraiths reported that at least thirty had become Zijin. And the number was steadily rising.

The lights were off in the truck. Only what moonlight filtered through the falling snow allowed Bishop to see. And that was all he needed. A small wraith, he looked no more than ten years old, shuffled cautiously up to the truck in the darkness. His fragile image trembled as the snow fell through him. His face was pale and his once fierce green eyes were flat and cold. He drifted up to the driver's side window. Bishop rolled the window down.

"We found her," he said.

Jordan fought to stay awake as his Jeep rolled to a stop at the intersection of Wichita and Cross. It had already been the longest day of his life and it wasn't even six o'clock. Since Sean awoke this morning in the good doctor's office he had seen and done things he never thought he'd do in Danaid, or anywhere else for that matter. His mind drifted backward through the day and the images he had seen. At the time he thought he would never sleep again. He had stayed wired and alert riding a powerful wave of adrenaline and fear, but even that wave couldn't last forever. He felt wrung out and done. All he wanted was to get home to his own bed and crash. His eyelids felt as heavy as lead weights. His head had been bobbing the whole way from the police station. He told himself he was only three blocks away, but even that felt too far.

Finally, his eyes slid shut. Garth Brooks sang somewhere far away. A horn's beep behind him snapped his head up. He glanced in his rearview, then up at the green light and pulled out.

Halfway through the intersection, a pickup truck nearly tore his front end off. Running straight through the red light it never even braked. Jordan slammed on the brakes and skidded to a stop, watching the maniac go. "Jesus Christ on a crutch!" he cursed, fully awake now after a sudden hit of adrenaline.

In the middle of the intersection with cars honking as they pulled around him, Jordan nervously grabbed his radio and called it in. A moment later Jordan hit the siren and the lights and tore up the street after the pickup.

Violet tiptoed into her spare bedroom and gently shook Sean awake.

"Sean? Sean?" she whispered. He awoke with a start.

"What is it? What's wrong?"

"Kelly's on the phone for you," she said. "Says Jordan found Norman's truck."

Sean jumped out of bed and blew past Violet out into the hall. He grabbed the phone from where it lay on the kitchen counter.

"Where is he?"

"He's at Fourth and Howard, heading north. It looks like Mulberry Road."

"Tell him I'm coming. Tell him not to do anything till I get there. You hear me, Kelly? Nothing," Sean said and slammed the phone down.

He raced for the door. He slipped on his boots, grabbed his coat and he was gone.

From the bedroom window, Kevin watched his dad's Jeep back out of the drive and disappear down the street.

CHAPTER 26

Petra stopped in the textured darkness of the forest. Moonlight sifted through the knotted canopy above, lending a silvered edge to the bark of the shadowed trees. Behind her, Zijin panted softly in the hushed silence, their hot breath smoking in the frozen air. Their lean, muscled bodies were ready to begin again their trek through the thigh-high snow on her word.

It was true that Petra was a door, but she was also a vessel, a life raft for the Zijin race. Inside her she carried the entire population of the doomed species. They had moved through worlds for centuries, like parasites, an infection or a virus. They spread from human to human, converting as many as possible. For every converted human allowed a Zijin to once again know life. Petra closed her eyes and listened. The sleepers, the waiting ones, called for her. Their cries begged for awakening.

Suddenly, she cut to her right, tearing through the fence of trees, gripping thin branches to pull herself forward even faster. Behind her the Zijin grunted with the effort. The impenetrably dark forest lightened as they approached the edge of the wood, where fluorescent light illuminated the knotted trunks.

Petra stopped at the edge of the darkness just inside the tree line and looked out over the expanse of yard.

A large red barn blocked most of the house from view. Behind it, firewood had been cut and stacked neatly against the back wall. A blue tarp was draped over the pile, doing its best to keep the wood out of the elements. An axe was wedged deep into the large stump nearby, which had been used as a chopping block. With the barn as cover, Petra and the Zijin broke from the tree line. As Petra passed the woodpile, she pulled the axe easily out of the stump.

Tammy Matthews stood next to her mother, shivering in the doorway. Her thin arms wrapped around herself. Her cotton Spice Girls pajamas just weren't enough against the bitter cold and the gusts of wind that found their way inside.

"What is he doing out there?" she asked, her teeth chattering. Martha Matthews leaned outside, her hands wrapped around a mug of hot coffee, and called out, "C'mon, Frank, the movie's coming on."

Tammy moved from the doorway to the window in the laundry room where she could see her dad, smoking his nightly cigar, a wine-tipped job that mom couldn't stand, as he flooded the backyard ice rink with a garden hose. Meanwhile her fourteen-year-old brother Jamie skated in circles around the hockey net, his feet crossing over gracefully as he made the tight circle. He cruised in front of the goal and ripped a puck over the strapped-in plastic goalie's right shoulder.

"Just a few more minutes, Mom, okay?" Jamie replied, digging the puck out of the net and skating hard to the edge of the ice. Stopping on a dime, he spun and fired a slapshot that rang right off the goalie's head and went straight up into the night air.

"Go ahead, hon," Frank said, with a wink and a smile as he swept the spray from his hose from side to side. "We'll be right there."

Martha returned the smile and said "all right," but soon her smile faded. Frank watched her smile dissolve and followed her stare over his right shoulder into the darkness around the barn.

Frank pinched off the hose and listened. He took a step toward the barn and waited. Skeins of snow blew across the open field into the black woods. Nothing there but shadows. But then the shadows moved. Three of them materialized out of the dark, scrambling down the side of the barn like spiders. As large as a man, they moved like animals, dropping gracefully into the snow from fifteen feet up.

Without taking his eyes away from the shadows, Frank called to his son. Jamie ripped a shot off the goal post and spun around toward his father.

"C'mon, Dad. I don't even care about the stupid movie."

"Jamie, goddammit, get in the house. Now."

Jamie stopped skating and looked at his dad staring off into the dark.

Three shapes scrambled over the snow, picking up speed, charging into the light.

"Dad? What is that?" Jamie asked, standing next to his father.

"Frank! Jamie! Get in the house right now!" Martha cried.

The sound of terror in Martha's voice ripped Frank from his stupor. As the first creature dipped its head into the light of the flood lamps, illuminating its terrible visage, he grabbed his son by the jacket and pulled him away across the ice.

Frank whispered. "Get in the house. As fast as you can."

Jamie took off like a shot, his thin legs pumping hard, his

skates tearing up the ice. Frank took off after him across the ice, that being the shortest distance between the two points.

His boots slipped across the slick surface as the night filled with the sounds of teeth chattering and nails scratching, digging into the ice.

Martha and Tammy screamed helplessly from the doorway. "C'mon, Dad, run!" And Frank ran. His legs pumped, his heart pounded. Frank slid through the layer of water he had just applied and fell heavily to his knees. He scrambled to his feet but fell again. Soaked and scared he crawled as fast as he could.

Jamie raced back out across the ice, head down, arms pumping, driving him forward.

"Jamie! Get back here!" Martha screamed from the doorway.

Frank looked up and got to his hands and knees. His family screamed for him to get up. He stole a glance over his shoulder. The creatures charged across the ice on all fours, their claws digging through the ice. Milky white skin, black eyes. Jaws ready to snap.

Jamie stopped hard next to his dad and grabbed his father's coat, pulling him to his feet.

The creatures leapt from the ice and tackled the two men together, knocking them clear into a drift and into the darkness. Frank and his son scrambled to their feet, kicking in the snow. Jamie screamed, a high-pitched shriek. And then there was silence as Jaime's scream was viciously cut short.

"Frank?"

"FRANK!" Martha screamed. But there was only darkness.

A woman emerged from the shadows and stepped into the

light of the ice rink. The hood of her coat hid the top part of her face but the woman's lips pulled into a smile. She held the axe in her right hand as she stepped toward the house.

"Mommy?" Tammy asked.

"Frank?"

The woman kept coming, slowly, deliberately.

"Frank!"

"Mommy?" Tammy pleaded.

Martha slammed the door and locked it. She spun away from the door and grabbed her daughter.

"Get upstairs, Tammy. Hurry."

"Mommy, where's daddy? Where's Jamie?" she asked, tears streaming down her cheeks. "Daddy!" she screamed.

Martha ran to the kitchen where she snagged the portable phone off the wall and dialed.

The phone was dead.

The windows shook in their frames as the creatures clambered over the glass, peering inside, watching the two women. Tammy screamed again as the monsters pressed close, their panting breath fogging up the glass. Their black eyes tracked them as the pair edged toward the stairs.

Suddenly, the blade of the axe bit through the back door. Martha screamed, dropped the phone and ran upstairs, pushing her daughter ahead of her every step of the way.

At the top of the stairs they followed the short hall to the left. Martha pulled Tammy along by the hand. The sound of breaking glass was everywhere as the creatures entered the home through the windows.

Martha yanked Tammy into a room near the end of the hall and eased the door closed.

Her husband, an amateur taxidermist and avid hunter, kept his trophies here. Stuffed ducks, geese, even a fox lined the blonde wood shelves. Martha headed straight for the gun cabinet. As she passed his worktable where an owl lay half completed, she grabbed a stone carving of a wolf and smashed the leftmost glass panel of the gun cabinet. Tammy stared in awe at her mother as she pulled down a shotgun from its rack and a box of shells.

"Get in that closet, honey," she said as she dumped the box of shells out on the floor and fed them into the chamber.

"Mommy, please," Tammy whined as she clung to her mother's side like an infant.

"It's going to be all right, Tammy."

Suddenly the house was thrown into darkness as the power was cut. Tammy screamed, throwing herself into her mother's arms. Martha set down the shotgun and rocked her daughter gently. She whispered low and fast, "Tammy, Tammy, quiet, honey, okay, please, you got to be quiet. I need you to be brave right now. Can you be brave? Can you be brave for me right now?"

Tammy nodded weakly, staring up into her mother's dark brown eyes.

"Okay. We'll both be brave, okay?"

"Okay," Tammy whispered.

Martha let Tammy go and she slid into place beside her mother. Huddled on the floor they listened to the darkness as Martha slid the remaining shells into the pockets of her jeans.

Beyond the door, the hardwood floor creaked as footsteps shuffled toward them. Claws scratched the plaster in the hall and the creatures chittered in their rattling machine gun language.

"Get behind me," Martha whispered. Tammy did what she was told and slid across the floor where she crawled behind her mother. Martha raised the shotgun. The barrel pointed at the center of the door. The footsteps drew closer.

Bishop slid all over the road, struggling to control the speed through the drifted streets of Danaid. Oliver rode shotgun. He peered through the windshield and the whipping snow. Wraiths had lined the street and converged on the farm house at the end of a long drive.

The headlights of the pickup swept over a row of mailboxes at the end of the driveway and Oliver shouted, "There! Turn right there!"

Bishop cranked the wheel and the truck spun nearly 360 degrees. Charging through the snow behind him was the sheriff's Jeep. Bishop had nowhere to go. The Jeep T-boned the pickup, driving it straight off the road and into the ditch. Bishop was thrown against the window, shattering the glass with his head.

Both vehicles came to a stop, blocking the narrow driveway. Gun up and ready, the deputy slid across the hood of his Jeep and dropped into the ditch next to the smashed window in the pickup. Bishop came around, slumped against the broken window.

"Let me see your hands! Show me your fucking hands!" the deputy said.

Bishop turned his face to the young deputy, blood streaming down into his right eye from a gash on his forehead.

"Get your fucking hands up! Now!" the deputy said. "Do it!"

The deputy cocked the hammer of his pistol and took aim at Bishop's head through the broken glass.

Bishop pressed his hands against the window glass as the deputy opened the door, backed up a few feet and said, "Okay. Nice and slow, get out of the truck."

Bishop did as he was told. The gash on his forehead had stopped bleeding as it sealed quickly.

"Listen to me, boy," Bishop whispered.

"Shut the fuck up and lean against the truck. Hands on the hood."

Bishop turned to the truck and the deputy pushed him into the position. As he went for his handcuffs with his right, Bishop spun and grabbed the deputy's gun hand. With his wrist pinned, the deputy fired harmlessly into the truck's engine block. In the next instant Bishop drove an elbow into the deputy's face, knocking him flat.

Bishop threw the deputy's gun into the ditch as headlights swept over him. He turned to see Sean coming up the driveway, already jumping out of his seat. Bishop ran toward the Matthews' house.

Sean was a few seconds too late. His Jeep skidded to a halt ten feet from the blockade that the other two vehicles had created. He ran down the driveway shouting, "Freeze! Freeze!" But Bishop didn't stop. Sean stopped, skidding in the snow. He shouted once more for him to freeze and then he took aim. The first shot was high, the second went off to the right, but the third slammed home, punching a fist-sized exit wound in Bishop's chest. His body was lifted off his feet and pitched forward into the snow where he skidded to a stop and didn't move.

Sean breathed hard as he ran to where Bishop lay.

"Stay down! Stay down! Show me your hands!"

Bishop didn't move. Sean dropped a knee down hard into the middle of his back and roughly cuffed Bishop's hands together. He rolled Bishop onto his back. The snow beneath him was stained red. He pulled apart Bishop's shirt. An angry red eye slowly closed in Bishop's pale chest.

"Jesus Christ," Sean whispered.

"You don't know what you're chasing," Bishop said, as blood spilled from the corner of his mouth.

"I found what I'm looking for."

Jordan came to a skidding stop beside Sean and stared down at Bishop, cuffed and bloody.

"You all right?" Sean asked.

"Yeah," Jordan replied absently. "Jesus, you shot him."

Sean nodded.

"Why is he cuffed?"

"'Cause he's not dead."

Jordan knelt down close to Bishop's head and felt for a pulse.

"He's dead, Sean."

Sean pushed him roughly away, down into the snow.

"Keep away from him!" Sean said. "Don't touch him. You hear me?"

"Jesus, Sean. He's dead," Jordan replied. "No pulse. Nothing."

"He's not dead," he said. "I don't know what he is." Sean grabbed Bishop by his ankles and dragged him back to his Jeep.

"Sean, what the fuck is going on?"

"He's not dead. He may look dead, but he's not!"

"Sean, you shot him through the chest, there's blood everywhere, he's got no pulse. He's gone."

Sean dropped Bishop into the snow, knelt down and tore open his blood soaked shirt.

"Look!" Sean said. "Where's the wound? Where'd I shoot him?"

Jordan stared at what remained of the bullet wound, a small red scar turning to pink just above Bishop's right nipple.

"Oh, my God."

"Listen to me. I saw this guy take a butcher knife to the throat and walk away. I don't—I don't know what's going on or what he is."

Jordan couldn't take his eyes away from Bishop's chest as the pink blemish of the bullet wound faded to pale white skin.

"What do we do?"

"Mom?" Tammy whispered. Her mother held a finger to her lips.

"Who's shooting?"

Tammy and her mother had heard three quick gunshots, then nothing.

"Quiet, Tammy."

"Is it Dad?" she whispered.

In the darkness of the den Martha could just make out the metal doorknob, glinting in the weak light. She watched it twist, its old mechanism creaking in the silence as it was wrenched from side to side. Martha's finger slid into the trigger guard, resting on the trigger.

Martha's body tensed as someone threw their shoulder into

the door. It buckled under the strain and rattled in its frame. Again and again the door was attacked. The weak light below the door flickered with every hit.

"Mommy?"

Suddenly the door was silent. The knob hung bent in its socket, but the siege had ended. Martha's arms trembled from holding the shotgun.

"Is it gone?"

Martha turned to find her daughter's pale face in the gloom, tear-stained and afraid. An axe blade sliced through the door nearly shearing it in half.

Martha spun and fired wildly. For a moment the door and the shining blade of the axe were illuminated in the muzzle flash. A pale hand snaked through the rent in the door to pull the axe head free. Martha aimed at the hand and fired and fired and fired. Tammy screamed but her voice was obliterated by the thunder of the shotgun blasts.

When Martha ran out of shells, heavy smoke hung around the two of them like a fog bank. As the echoes faded along with the smoke, Martha and Tammy looked at the remains of their only defense. The door to the den hung limply by one hinge.

"Get in the closet, Tammy," her mother whispered.

Martha was on her hands and knees fumbling in the dark, digging through the pockets of her jeans for the remaining shells. She fed them in one at a time, scanning the darkness as Tammy clung to her side.

"Tammy, please."

"No, Mommy, no," Tammy whispered. "Come with me, we can hide."

"Get in that closet now. I'm not going to tell you again," Martha whispered fiercely. "Do it, Tammy."

Tammy crawled away crying, her wet breath coming out in sobs. The closet door scraped against the carpet as Tammy opened it and slid inside. With the shotgun loaded Martha moved backwards until her back was against the closet door. She felt Tammy's little fingers through the wooden slats. Tammy cried softly.

"Mommy, I'm scared, please, stay with me, please."

Moonlight dimly lit the hall and the edge of the doorframe. There was no sound. Martha raised the shotgun at the doorway and wondered how long she could hold out. The box of shells was empty and she would never be able to find more in the dark. She had to make each one count.

Fingernails scraped across wood and her eyes snapped open in the darkness. Somewhere close she could hear breathing, quick and deep, like the panting of an animal.

"Mom?"

The shotgun blasts sent Sean diving for the ground and froze Jordan standing in place.

"Jordan! Get down!" Sean said.

Jordan hit the ground looking ashen.

"What the hell is going on?" he asked. "Who's shooting?"

"It came from inside," Sean said.

"What are they shooting at?"

"I don't know."

Sean rose into a crouch and scanned the front of the house.

"What do we do?" asked Jordan, as he belly-crawled closer

to Sean.

"There could be more people in there."

"No shit," Jordan said.

"More of his people," Sean said as he nodded toward Bishop, still lying flat on his back in the snow.

"Oh, Jesus Christ, you never said he had partners," Jordan said.

"He could have," Sean said. "I just didn't see them."

"We gotta get help then. We gotta—"

"There is no help," Sean said. "We're it. There's only us."

"I can't go in,"

"These are your people in there. The Matthews, remember?"

"I don't even have a gun."

Sean removed his back-up piece from his ankle holster and gave it to Jordan.

"There."

Jordan held the snub-nosed .38 tight to his chest and got to his feet.

"You ready?" Sean said.

Jordan nodded, "What about him?"

Sean and Jordan dragged Bishop's lifeless body to a low, wrought iron fence and secured him to it with Jordan's cuffs.

Sean took the right side of the house and agreed to meet Jordan in the backyard. Quickly he assessed the extent of the attack on the house. Windows were smashed, deep claw marks gouged the wood trim, and from what he could see through the broken windows, it looked as if a bomb had gone off inside. Furniture was scattered and toppled, plaster hung in chunks from the ceiling.

When they found each other in the backyard, Sean pointed his flashlight into the house and led them through the shredded back door.

Inside, all was still.

"Frank?" he called.

Snow had blown inside, covering the first twenty feet of the floor in a thin blanket of white. Sean listened to the house groan against the force of the wind and the snow outside and then led them deeper into the darkness of the house.

"Frank? Tammy? It's Sean."

Sean and Jordan made quick work of the ground floor, sweeping their lights over every surface and into every corner, but there was no sign of anyone.

They were halfway up the stairs when they heard the sound, low and indistinct at first but gradually louder. Sean thought it was the sound of hushed conversation. They moved forward.

Outside, Bishop slowly joined the living once again. Faraway he heard the howl of the freezing wind, and the brittle sound of barren branches shaking against each other. Then came the tactile senses; the bone deep cold of lying prone in the snow, the sharp little daggers of snow and ice hitting his face. Bishop's eyes slid open.

He found Oliver squatting over him.

"Welcome back, lad," he said. "Come on now, no rest for the wicked."

On the second floor, Sean's light found the study door hanging by a single hinge. Sean and Jordan stepped to the doorway and moved inside. Nearly everything was destroyed.

Hunks of plaster were scattered everywhere as was most of the furniture and a blizzard of glass. Again, deep claw marks gouged the wood floor and the walls, even the ceiling. Wordlessly the pair stepped back out into the hall and made their way to the end of the hall to the master bedroom. Sean felt Jordan behind him, less than a foot back. He hoped that he wouldn't catch an accidental bullet in the spine from his thoroughly spooked deputy.

As Sean reached for the doorknob to the master bedroom, the buzz of hushed conversation abruptly died. As if someone had thrown a switch, the sound stopped. Sean and Jordan stopped dead. Sean wrapped his gloved hand around the doorknob and Jordan grabbed his arm, shaking his head vehemently, pulling Sean away from the door. But Sean wouldn't budge. He peeled off Jordan's hand and motioned for him to be quiet. Jordan took a step backwards into the hall and Sean turned back to the door. The knob turned and the door swung inward.

Sean's flashlight cut through the gloom of the bedroom and found that all the furniture had been pushed to the far end of the room. Nothing remained, except for the two naked figures that lay curled on the floor. The air wheezed out of Jordan's lungs, something between a sigh and a groan. Sean stepped into the room, his feet reluctantly sliding across the hardwood. Martha lay curled on her side, facing the door, but it wasn't Martha. Not anymore. Her skin looked gray and cracked like desert hardpan shot through with intricate networks of black veins. What could only be her daughter Tammy lay partly behind her, curled almost in a fetal position with her knees drawn up to her thin chest.

"Oh, Jesus," Sean whispered.

Jordan pulled his radio from his belt.

"I'm calling the doc."

He squeezed the TALK button.

"Kelly, come in," Jordan whispered.

Nothing but static.

"Kelly, come in, over."

Sean moved slowly to the shivering form of Martha Matthews. Her eyes were closed but moved rapidly left to right beneath her thin lids. He brushed her once blonde hair that had now gone gray, away from her throat. He pulled off his glove and touched two fingers to her throat to feel for a pulse.

"Don't touch it."

Sean and Jordan spun toward the door, guns up and aimed, to find Bishop leaning against the frame.

"Holy fuck!" Jordan said. "What the fuck are you?"

"Hands up! Now! On the ground!" Sean said.

Bishop took a last drag on his cigarette and crushed the butt against the doorframe.

"Jesus, we gonna do this shit again?"

"Tell me what's going on here," Sean said. "What did you do?"

"Me?" Bishop replied. "Not enough. Now get up and back away, slowly."

"These people need help," Sean said.

Bishop shook his head, "It's too late."

"Please," a voice whispered, "help me."

Sean turned to where Tammy lay. Jordan and Bishop stepped closer.

A sound like ice breaking came from Tammy's body. She

rolled onto her back and whipped back her head, her back arched, and her body went rigid, as if she were in the midst of a powerful seizure. Her mouth and eyes snapped open. Her blue eyes stared blindly at the ceiling for a moment and then with the sound of tearing leather, her gray skin ripped down the center of her, from her navel to her throat. Her jaws clamped shut, cracking her teeth and leaving fragments to litter the floor beside her head. A molar rolled toward Jordan's boot and he scrambled away from it.

"Jesus Christ! What the fuck is happening?" Jordan asked Bishop.

"There's no time," Bishop replied. "We have to leave."

Tammy rolled to her stomach then snapped into a crouch. Her blue eyes faded to a milky white only to be filled from within, as if a viscous black fluid was pumped into her eyes until the solid white orbs darkened to a deep coal-black stare. Black markings moved under her skin, swirling and covering her body with strange, writhing symbols.

Bishop raised his gun and fired, obliterating the left side of Tammy's head. She was thrown backward where she landed in a heap. Her limbs shuddered against the floor as her life drained away.

Bishop took aim at Martha slowly getting to her feet.

"No," Sean said, as he stepped into the line of fire.

"Look at her, Sean," Bishop said. "They are not the people you knew. They're not your friends. We have no time to fuck around here."

Behind Sean, behind Martha, lay the large bay window of the master bedroom. Bishop saw them a moment too late. Fists cocked, mouths open, the Zijin smashed through the window and flooded the bedroom in a blizzard of thrashing limbs, glass and shrieks.

CHAPTER 27

The Rolling Stones were just finishing up "Brown Sugar" as Violet added the last of the chocolate chips to the batter. Violet's feet tapped but she didn't sing along. Classic rock and baking high-calorie treats was how she got through things. That and a box of tissue about every ten feet.

She had just finished mixing the last of the ingredients when the power went out.

"Shit."

Kevin could hear Violet rummaging through drawers and slamming cabinet doors. Finally a ray of light shot into the living room. She spent the next few minutes searching for matches with the assistance of her new-found flashlight.

"Violet?" Kevin asked from the darkened living room.

"It's okay, honey," she said, "power's out."

Violet peered out through the new snow down the length of Main Street. The whole town was dark.

If this kept up for any length of time they would start ringing the bell for everyone to come to the church. Violet didn't want to risk it. Not with Kevin. The winters here could be brutal and with no power the temperature inside her little storefront house would drop like a rock.

Up the street near Mabel's, something dashed across the street. She pressed her cheek to the window to get a better look but it was gone. Fast, she thought. Too big to be a dog. Dog wouldn't last very long out there tonight. Not much would. Weatherman said the temperature would fall to about –39, without the windchill, before the night was through. Violet took another look down both ends of the street and then set about to look for candles and matches.

"Looks like no cookies tonight, Kev."

"That's okay," he said, "but now what are we gonna do?"

"We're gonna pack your stuff and I'm gonna pack a bag and then we're gonna head over to the church."

"What are we gonna do there?"

"You play Monopoly?"

"No one beats me at Monopoly."

Violet laughed. "Oh, is that right?"

"It's a fact."

"Sounds like a challenge."

"Bring it."

"You wait right there," Violet said. She tossed the dishtowel at Kevin and then whirled away, disappearing with a long blue candle clenched in her fist.

Kevin threw his things into his backpack. He didn't have much; his PSP, a few scattered games. All his clothes had been packed already in anticipation of the power outage, so after a few quick looks around the general area to see if he'd missed anything, he was good to go. He couldn't wait to beat Violet at Monopoly. His smile returned at the prospect. She had no idea what she was up against.

He moved to the long windows and scanned the eerily darkened Main Street. The street looked like a view to another world, empty and desolate. He cupped his hands around his face to see more clearly and stared into the face of what lay curled and ready to pounce just beyond the windowpane.

Before he could scream, the pale creature drove its fist through the thin barrier between them. Kevin leapt backward, stumbled over his own feet and dropped to the floor. Long black talons eager for flesh snapped at Kevin's face and chased him backward. Kevin scrambled to his feet and backpedaled as fast as his feet would take him, never taking his eyes from the window. He slammed hard into Violet as she hurried into the room, brought by the sound of shattering glass. Her scream caught in her throat.

At the window the beast struggled to pull its arm free. Finally, it wrenched the arm out through the jagged hole, shredding its pale flesh and splashing the hardwood with its blood. The creature roared and then slammed itself bodily through the window in a blizzard of broken glass.

Shards of glass fell inward as the creature stepped into the living room. Violet yanked Kevin into her arms and started for the stairs. She took them two at a time. At the top of the stairs Violet's wheezing sounded like the high, thin scream of a boiling kettle. She nearly slipped on the area rug at the top of the steps, but stumbling, she managed to get to the only room with a lock, the bathroom.

She deposited Kevin into the clawfoot tub and slammed the door behind them, slipping the bolt through the cradle. She dragged over a high armoire and wedged it between the door and the sink. The piece was her mother's and made of oak, but it wasn't exactly a butcher's block. She prayed that it would hold. She searched for a weapon when the first attack came. The lock was torn from the wall and the door swung inward about three inches before the armoire stopped it.

In the tub, with his thin arms wrapped around his knees,

Kevin was as silent as a statue. Violet swept through items kept in boxes beneath the sink and came out with a curling iron and a small pair of scissors.

The door shook and splintered with each attack. Hinges pulled out of the wall. The armoire cracked, the tiny spindles snapped like toothpicks.

Violet slipped into the tub behind Kevin, wrapped her arms around him and prayed.

Gertie arrived at the church feeling deflated and physically gutted by what she had seen at the Walters' house. Normally a free thinker and an even freer speaker, her silence and reticence were duly noted. She endured polite jabs and then later heartfelt enquiries as to her health or some other dreaded secret that kept her tongue silenced the entire afternoon. There were reasons why she kept quiet, but those were her own. Everyone didn't have to know everything. Besides, she just didn't want to talk about it. To even think about it brought the taste of fresh bile to the back of her throat. She just wanted to keep busy, to be doing something instead of sitting home doing crosswords or watching some old movie. She wanted to be here. Doing. And she was. Presently she stirred a huge pot of chicken noodle soup. She added a little salt and kept stirring.

For a while she was worried that she had made the wrong decision. That was until the power went out. It went out every year, but never for this long. Father Callahan had waited for a couple of hours to pass before he had rung the emergency siren. Now he rang it once an hour.

She had heard a crew had been sent. It was usually Kelly

Dugan, or John Carney, the local electricians, and a few of their buddies to help them drink along the way out to the power station, but they left hours ago. No one asked where they had gotten to, or why it was taking so long. They were used to everything taking a little longer out here in the sticks, and even longer still during a storm. That was why no one panicked except for Gertie. That was why she was scared like she had never been before. Her stomach churned like an angry sea.

"Soup about ready?" a voice asked.

Gertie turned and found Hazel Klens' smiling face a couple of inches from her own. Hazel's left eye was punctured and smeared across her face like so much egg yolk. Her gray tweed suit was shredded, ripped up the front, and her pale, fish-belly skin was exposed, splattered with dark crimson. Organs spilled to the floor between broken ribs, skittering across the worn linoleum.

"Gertie?" Hazel asked, "Everything all right?"

Gertie's vision swam for a moment and then focused on Hazel's face. She wore too much foundation, and her eyebrows were in need of a good plucking, but other than that her face was as complete and as benign as it always was.

Hazel's pinched expression of concern dissolved into a smile as Gertie spoke.

"Sorry, Hazel," she said. "Daydreaming, I guess."

"Well, there's no time for that today," Hazel announced. "We have a few more hungry mouths to feed out there."

"More?"

Hazel nodded happily as if she were the owner of a new restaurant enjoying a packed house on opening night.

"The Larkins, the Shabos, and the Frys just arrived, hungry of course. That brings the total to fifty-four."

"Any word on Kelly's crew?" Gertie asked.

"I think so," Hazel replied. "I think Mr. Tremblay was talking to him on one of them walkie-talkie thingies."

"So," Gertie asked, "what's the status? When will the power be back on?"

"Oh, I don't know, Gertie," Hazel said. "I'm not good with the technical hullaballoo."

Gertie stepped out of her way as she brought down a few more bowls from a cupboard and set them on a serving tray.

CHAPTER 28

Kelly slammed the phone down into the cradle.

"Shit!"

The battery-powered emergency lights sprang to life but that was it. No computers, no coffee machine, no heat, and now, no phone. She couldn't even get a dial tone.

She took a few deep breaths and tried to calm down. It sucks, but don't lose it, was her mantra. It sucks—and she couldn't get farther than that. She took comfort in the fact that she knew in her heart that as soon as the power outage occurred, Kelly Dugan would be called and already on his way to the power station. No need to worry. She'll be back up in no time. What's the worst thing that happened? She thought it through. She didn't get to save her last game of Tetris on her computer before the blackout. She figured she would probably be able to go and live a normal life after the initial shock of it was over. She chuckled at her own circumstance.

She scooped the tennis ball off the ground, slipped on her glove and whipped a strike at the wall where poor defenseless Smokey the Bear took the ball squarely between the eyes.

"What are you doing?" Norman asked from the darkness of his cell.

Kelly didn't respond but she could hear the old man's feet scrape across the floor as he shifted position in his cell. By the groan of metal she knew he was leaning against the bars by the door of the cell.

"Kelly."

His voice was closer now.

"I'm not talking to you," she replied.

"We have to get to the shelter. St. Patrick's church."

"I know where the shelter is. You don't gotta tell me where the shelter is. I know where the goddamn shelter is, Norman."

"Kelly, are you listening?" Norman asked, "We have to—"

"I don't have to do anything but sit and wait. You have to shut up or I'll cuff you to my Jeep outside."

Norman watched Kelly toss the ball at the poster on the wall a few more times and then tried again.

"Kelly."

This time she spun in her seat and glared at him in the near dark.

"What?" she snapped.

"This blackout is not going to end."

"Why? How do you know?" she asked, "You do it? You sabotage the power station?" She smiled at her little joke and resumed tossing and catching her tennis ball.

"No. But—"

There was no easy way to explain to someone, especially someone as obtuse as Kelly Fike, that during his brief incarceration he had been visited in his cell by a wraith by the name of Jeremiah Colt, a gold miner who died in the Monk's Head Mine cave-in of 1966. There was no easy way to tell her that Jeremiah had informed him that the power would remain out because there was no longer a power station, just the twisted burning hulk that remained after the explosion. The Zijin had taken care of that.

"There's no way you can possibly predict how long the power is going to be out. You might as well give it up 'cause we're not going anywhere. We're just gonna sit here and wait," she said. "And if you're real quiet until the power comes back on, I mean silent, and I'm talking so quiet I get lulled into thinking I'm all alone in here quiet, then I'll make you a hot chocolate. Okay?"

"We're going to freeze," Norman replied, zipping his coat up to his throat.

"We'll be fine," Kelly replied.

She shivered, but didn't reach for her coat. Not yet. It wasn't that cold. Besides, she wouldn't want to give the old son of a bitch the satisfaction. She wheeled her tennis ball at the wall and snatched it out of the air with a satisfying slap of leather.

"What about Ruby?"

"There goes your hot chocolate."

"I'm serious, what about Ruby?"

"What about her?"

"She'll freeze out there at the house in the dark."

"She'll be fine.'

"She'll die, Kelly."

"Relax, Norman."

"How long are you gonna wait? Until Jordan gets back?" Norman asked. "What if he never makes it back?"

"Okay, I'm serious now," Kelly said, pulling the ball into her glove one last time and then getting to her feet. "I've talked to you enough for today. Shut up now."

"We have to get to the shelter and we have to save Ruby."

"You're not the boss of me, you know! You're not!"

"I know. I know. Just please, listen. Help me. Save my dog, save Ruby, please! Please! Leave me here if you want to. Handcuff me. You know me, I'm not a criminal. Please, Kelly."

Kelly had never been a dog person and even if she were, it was doubtful that she would take a criminal suspect like Norman out into the storm to save his dog. She thought about it briefly, but she never, not for a second, thought the power would remain off for more than an hour.

After the first hour, Kelly took to standing by the front door. By now she was dressed in her winter coat, boots, gloves and toque. She shuffled side to side to stay warm, but it didn't do much good as the temperature plummeted inside the police station. Kelly took one more long look in both directions down the darkened street, and when she found nothing but darkness and blowing wind, she turned away from the window.

She scratched out a quick note to Sean and Jordan, outlining her intentions, and left it taped to the inside of the front door window.

Norman was bundled up tight in blankets she had found piled in a closet near the bathroom. He was silent, but he had already said everything he had to.

"You ready?" she asked.

Norman nodded and pulled himself free of his blanket cocoon just in time to catch a pair of handcuffs Kelly sailed through the bars. He gave her a questioning look.

"Wear them or stay here," she said. "It's up to you."

Norman slipped the metal cuffs over his wrists and stood in front of the cell door.

Kelly drove slowly to begin with, but now, in the blowing snow, where no sane person would even think of venturing outside, they were barely moving.

She knew that the wrought iron fence that bordered the cemetery stood buried in snow less than twenty feet to her right, but she couldn't see it.

"It's right up here," Norman assured her.

"You been sayin' that for the last twenty minutes."

"The way you drive," Norman whispered under his breath.

"You wanna get out and walk, be my guest."

Kelly puttered on through the snow and Norman stayed quiet for another minute, his nose pressed to the cold glass.

"There," he said, "Turn right here."

Kelly slowly made the turn and as the driveway rose to meet her she made out the general shape of Norman's house. She pulled up as close as possible to the front door and parked.

"Stay here."

"What?"

"I said, stay here." Kelly repeated. "I'll be right back."

"But I have to go, I have to see her, I—"

Kelly turned to Norman, "You want your dog or not?"

Norman nodded.

"Stay here."

Kelly braced herself against the cold and then stepped out into the storm. The wind was so strong it was a struggle to get her door open. She stepped into the knee-deep snow. Wind instantly gutted her of any warmth she brought with her and stung her face and cheeks. With her head bent into the wind, she trudged through the drifts to Norman's front door.

She pulled a flashlight out of her holster. She tried the doorknob, found it open and stepped in.

Inside, Kelly got a sickening feeling of déjà vu. She did not want to find anyone in here besides the damn dog. She swept her light from left to right over the tiled floor of the mudroom and called.

"Ruuuuu-beeeeee! Come here, girl!"

She waited, just inside the door, just deep enough to allow the door to close behind her. She did not want to search the house looking for some senile old dog that was probably cowering under a bed somewhere.

"Ruby! Come on now!"

Where the hell was that dog?

She took a step into the main living area and let her flashlight play over the kitchen table, the counter, the remnants of breakfast still left out: a peanut butter jar, a tomato, a few dirty plates and a coffee mug. Suddenly she was hungry.

Damn dog.

"Ruby!" she cried. "Come on, let's go you stupid mutt!"

Kelly checked her watch. It had taken over an hour to get here. More than likely it would take at least another hour to get to the church. She was starving. As if on cue, her stomach grumbled noisily.

In the fridge she found a few loose pepperoni sticks and a brick of havarti cheese. No reason not to have a little snack, she figured. After all, she was doing old Norman a pretty big favor driving out here on the outskirts of town looking for his stupid dog. No reason at all. She leaned against the counter and took a bite of the dried pepperoni. Delicious. She slipped a slice of cheese into her mouth and then she heard it.

She stopped chewing and listened. There it was again, a moan, a soft whimper. What if Ruby is hurt? Or caught? That would mean going upstairs, by herself. Suddenly she thought that forcing Norman to stay in the Jeep was the biggest mistake she could have made. She grabbed up the remaining pepperoni and the brick of cheese and slipped it into a crisper near the top in the fridge. She then took a step toward the front door. She heard the sound again. This time there was no mistaking it. It was pain. And it came from upstairs.

❧

Ten minutes later Norman still stared at his front door from the Jeep.

"What the hell is taking so long?"

He swiveled in his seat to look down the length of the driveway, but the snow had covered the rear window. He went back to his view out his window and came face to face with his mother.

"Jesus Christ!" he shrieked, reeling back across the seat. "You gotta stop doing that," he said. "Jesus, you'd think I'd get used to it."

His mother's face looked grim and afraid.

"Go, Norman," she said. "Go. Right now."

"I can't go. Kelly Fike is in there getting Ruby. Besides I—"

"They're gone, Norman," his mother said. "Gone."

His mother turned toward the house, fear rippling her features.

"Just trust me and go!" she said just below a scream, "Go!"

Norman couldn't think. Dead? Gone?

"Go!"

Where could he go? He was locked in the back seat of a police Jeep. Norman knew better than to argue with his mother, but he was trapped. Between the back seat and the front was a metal grill bolted to the Jeep's frame. He wasn't getting through that.

He peered outside into the blowing snow at his front door, praying that his mother was wrong and Kelly and Ruby would

step out into the snow. But the door remained closed.

"Go, Norman!"

Norman cursed. He would be upset later, right now he was just really really pissed. He rolled onto his back and brought his boots up against the window glass. He drew back his knees and drove his boot heels at the window. The rebound sent what felt like shards of glass up his legs into his arthritic hips. He whimpered, but he had a feeling that was the best it was gonna get. He drew back his knees again and this time he gave it all he had. The glass cracked. He kicked the pane again and his boot-clad feet burst through the shattered glass.

"Hurry," his mother urged.

"Okay! Okay!" he hissed. "I'm nearly seventy, you know."

Norman adjusted himself on the car seat so he could poke his head out through the broken window. He reached up to the roof and grabbed the roof rack. He pulled on the roof rack and got himself to a sitting position on the window ledge. He tried pulling his right foot out through the window but he wasn't that limber.

"Come on!" she cried. "They're coming!"

Norman's head whipped toward the front door. He couldn't see anyone, but it didn't make him feel any better. He let go of the roof rack and let himself fall backwards into the snowdrift. He scrambled to his feet and then to the driver's side door. For a sickening moment, Norman was sure he had watched Kelly lock her driver's door. He tried the handle and the door swung open. He slipped behind the wheel and dropped the shift into reverse. With his foot on the brake he took one long last look at the front door. He believed his mother, but he still felt guilty leaving Kelly and Ruby.

His eye registered movement, a flickering shadow over the hood of the Jeep. As Norman looked up through the windshield, the creature dropped onto the hood with a crash. Snarling and snapping, the Zijin scratched at the windshield, gouging the glass with its talons.

Norman stepped on the gas and the Jeep lurched backwards. The Zijin held fast. It cocked its arm back and drove a ham-sized fist through the windshield. Long, black talons ripped at Norman's clothes. Its nails snapped and clawed as Norman cranked the wheel and hit the brakes, sending the Jeep into a spin. The Zijin was ripped from the hood of the car and tumbled through the snow. Norman hit the gas but went nowhere. He pressed the pedal but the Jeep's tires spun uselessly.

The hulking shape of the Zijin rose from the drifted snow and stepped casually toward the driver's side window. He wasn't alone. Another, smaller creature crept up. They were ten feet away and moving with purpose.

Norman pinned the gas pedal to the floor but the Jeep slid side to side as the tires spun, churning up clouds of white powder. He threw it in reverse and gunned the engine again. Snow and wind howled through the hole in the windshield. Norman was freezing, but he was too scared to care. His heart slammed against his chest. Each beat pounded in his ears. Sweat burned into his eyes. He gave up on reverse and dropped the stick shift into drive and gunned the engine again. The smaller Zijin was at his driver's side window, close enough to fog the window with its breath. Norman couldn't bring himself to look at the face staring at him. He knew if he did the night would be over. He wouldn't be able to move and he would crumble under its stare.

"Oh, Jesus Christ, oh, God …"

The creature snapped a punch at the window, spider-webbing the glass. Norman kept his foot pinned to the floor as the Jeep swung left to right wearing a groove into the snow.

The window exploded inches from his face. Norman pulled away, but he was yanked back as the Zijin's claws dug deep into the meat of his shoulder. Norman howled but never let his foot off the gas pedal. Blood sluiced down his sleeve, spreading across his chest and back. The creature's claws were like knives and twisted in the wound. His vision was clouded by stars. His head dipped as darkness took a swipe at him.

The Jeep lurched forward suddenly, breaking the Zijin's grip. The wheel spun in Norman's hands as the Jeep headed straight down the driveway toward the road. He cranked the wheel using his good arm and somehow managed to apply the brakes to make the turn onto the main road. He couldn't hear anything, he was screaming too loud.

Norman resisted the temptation to keep the gas pedal buried all the way back to town, for he knew that at his current speed he would no doubt end up in the ditch within five minutes. He eased up until he was at a manageable speed. He took a peek into the rearview and saw nothing but snow, ice and darkness.

He heard it first. The weight of the creature clinging to the roof buckled the metal. Claws scratched the metal skin of the hull. Norman couldn't take his eyes off the rearview mirror as a mini-horror movie spun through its final reel.

A pale claw slid through the broken back window, the window that he himself had broken to escape. Next came the sinuous forearm, heavily roped with thick cords of muscle.

He could jerk the wheel, hopefully dislodging the creature from the roof, without losing control of the Jeep, but the wheels were already slipping over the icy road. He could slam on the brakes. What he could not do was let the creature into the vehicle, where it could eviscerate him at its leisure from the back seat.

Norman slammed on the brakes and the Jeep went into a skid. The creature shrieked, and Norman hoped the evil son of a bitch was getting ripped apart. But Norman had to focus, the Jeep spun almost sideways. He steered into the skid and brought the Jeep back on track. He glanced at the rearview and didn't see a hand holding on. He took a breath.

"Oh, thank you Jesus."

He felt the creature's breath on his neck. He spun in his seat. The claw arced down toward him. Norman dove for the floorboards. The creature's claw buried itself deep into the headrest, missing Norman by inches.

The Zijin roared and ripped its claw free of the twisted mess of material and stuffing. The steering wheel wobbled on its own with no one at the helm. Norman stared up at the creature awaiting the final move when the front end of the Jeep suddenly dropped five feet. Norman's head smashed into the glove box and for a moment he felt pain and then there was nothing but darkness.

Norman awoke shaking. Blood trickled into his eye and down his cheek. His left shoulder throbbed. But he was alive, and that was something. He looked up. The Zijin had been thrown forward into the windshield. Its head and shoulders made it through the glass barrier, but the rest of it was still inside the Jeep.

Norman winced with every movement, but like it or not, he really didn't have a choice. He had to get out of there and far away in a hurry. He pulled himself up into the passenger seat and cranked down the window. The window was halfway down when he heard the creature stir. His head whipped around and the creature came back on line.

Thick branches of bone had been broken, some poking through the creature's massive back, dripping gore. Slowly, they returned to their original shape, repairing themselves, knitting together as if they had never broken.

Norman levered himself out through the window and into the snow. The cold was beyond freezing. It left freezing in the dust somewhere. This was different, even to Norman, who had spent his entire life here. His gloves and toque were inside the wreckage, or possibly back in his driveway, knocked loose when he fell out of the window. The point was, he was uncovered, certain to die out here if he didn't find shelter soon, whether the creature came after him or not.

He zipped his coat and held the throat closed. He tried to imagine where he was. Everything was white. There were no landmarks. All he had was his memory. Just below the torrents of wind came the whine of a snowmobile. He couldn't tell if it was approaching or even from what direction it was coming. He took his best guess and headed in that direction.

He was getting very tired from the intense cold and the blood loss and the shock of the last few minutes. He concentrated on lifting one foot and then the other. Left, right, left, right, over and over through the snow he trudged. Blood dripped from his mouth onto his clenched right fist. His right leg sank thigh-deep and he pitched forward. As if on cue the wind picked up, holding him down as a thin drift spun over him. He got back to his feet.

The creature flew out of the storm like a missile. Two hundred and fifty pounds of muscle slammed into his back, cracking ribs and pounding out his breath in one wheezing gasp.

Deep in the snow, Norman was on his back, trying desperately to beat away his attacker. Its claws dug into his biceps, crushing the fight out of him. The heavily muscled arms pinned his, like a jumble of sticks, close to his chest. Norman tried to scream, but he didn't have the breath. It was happening too fast. He couldn't think. His vision was failing, everything darkening. The beast thrust its head at Norman's throat.

His heart sounded like shotgun blasts in his ears.

Norman opened his eyes. He could breathe again, and the air above him was clear, full of big beautiful snowflakes. Another shotgun blast brought Norman to his knees. About ten feet to his left three men dressed in full snowmobile suits and ski masks surrounded the bleeding Zijin. The creature twitched as it died, its chest a gaping wound, its head obliterated above the eyes. One of the group stepped forward and pumped two more shells into the dying thing. The creature was dead. At least for now.

When Norman felt another's touch he jumped.

"Easy, there," the woman said. "It's all right."

Norman's eyes were wild and he had trouble focusing.

"You're Norman Conklin, right?" she asked.

Norman couldn't stop shaking. His eyes rolled up into his head and once again he slipped into the dark.

CHAPTER 29

The Zijin flooded through the bay window in a gray-skinned wave. Sean could barely see in the gloom, getting only snapshots of light as he and Bishop and Jordan fired their weapons.

Bishop yanked Sean out of the line of fire and killed the creature that had once been Martha Matthews. Next he drew a flare from a pocket of his coat and sparked it to life. Soon the room flickered in brilliant green light. Jordan couldn't stop screaming. He fired all six shots of his borrowed .38 and then threw the empty gun at the rushing horde. Bishop grabbed him by the arm and hauled him toward the door. Sean was already backing up, firing quick and sure. He hit a charging creature three times in the chest, but the Zijin kept coming.

"Gotta get 'em in the head to put them down," Bishop shouted.

Bishop fired his last round and popped the clip. Two Zijins charged him from the right before he had time to reload. Bishop flexed his right wrist outward and a seven-inch blade slid into his waiting palm. He sidestepped the pair and slashed the first one across the throat. The other lunged for Bishop and got six inches of his blade straight through its right eye.

Sean and Jordan stumbled out into the hallway. Bishop soon followed.

"Stay behind me," Bishop said.

Sean and Jordan followed Bishop down the hall to the stairs and toward the front door.

"No, wait!" Sean said. "This way!"

Bishop spun, "We got no time for this," he said. "We got to get out of here."

"We go out the front door we won't get ten feet."

Window glass shattered all around them in the dark as Zijin fought to get inside. But Sean dragged Jordan back into the house.

"This way!" Sean said.

Bishop took another look at the front door less than ten feet away then followed Sean. Sean felt his way down the narrow hall past the bathroom and the laundry room on the left. His hand passed over the doorjamb and then he found it. The metal door was cold. The knob turned and Sean pushed through into the Matthews' garage.

Just as he thought, the Matthews' rusted out Honda Civic and their newer Dodge Durango sat waiting. Blessedly, the keys were in the ignition.

"You drive," Sean said to Jordan.

"Me? Why?"

"Because with the power out we have to raise the door by hand."

Jordan looked to the wide garage door and paled. "Oh, shit."

Bishop moved to the front grill of the SUV.

"Soon as I start raising the door," Sean said to Jordan, "you rev that engine. We're gonna need a lot of speed out of the gate."

Jordan slid behind the wheel.

Sean looked to Bishop, holding a gun in each hand.

"You ready?"

Bishop nodded.

Sean positioned himself at the side of the garage door and with his gloved hands on the chains he nodded once and started pulling. The door raised an inch. It rattled and shook on its track as a crowd of Zijin threw themselves against it. Their claws slashed across the gap into the garage. Bishop fired and blasted fingers and hands to pieces.

Behind them the big V8 engine of the Durango revved to life.

Sean pulled the chains and watched helplessly as the door rose and the creatures poured through the gap. One slashed him across the hand before he could move. He reeled backward and the door dropped a good six inches. Blood from Sean's hand splattered across the cement floor and the garage door.

"Keep pulling!" shouted Bishop.

Sean snapped back to the chain and pulled harder than before. The door rose and he kicked and screamed at the approaching creatures. A Zijin lunged at Sean. Bishop fired, killing the beast, but not before its razored talon cut through Sean's jeans just above his knee. Sean fell. Bishop grabbed him before he hit the ground, leaning him against the inside of the garage. With one hand Bishop pulled on the chain, leaving his other hand to fire his weapon. When the door was nearly open all the way, Bishop dragged Sean back to the Durango and pushed him into the back seat. Bishop kept firing, keeping the creatures at bay, until his weapon was empty. Then it was a race. Bishop squeezed into the back seat behind Sean and closed the door. Instantly the window exploded inward as the Zijin rushed the truck and reached inside for its occupants.

"Go!" Bishop shouted.

Jordan dropped the SUV into drive. The big vehicle tore

through the crowd of Zijin and exploded out of the garage. The tires squealed and smoked as the Durango lurched forward through the tide of rushing Zijin. Showing no fear, the creatures charged the big SUV, leaping onto the hood, clinging to the roof rack. Jordan smashed through, cutting a swath through the crowd until he hit snow. Moving too fast to correct the skid, the Durango slid sideways. Jordan cranked the wheel and, with the tail end fishtailing, he maneuvered down the driveway.

Claws skittered across metal and glass. Through the blowing snow Jordan saw the glint of metal.

"Oh, fuck,"

There was a space on the left hand side between the Matthews' wrought iron fence and the two vehicles at the end of the driveway, but it was going to be tight. Jordan goosed the engine picking up speed going downhill.

"Hold on!" Jordan called, and headed for a gap that would be impossible to fit this full-sized SUV through.

"Oh, Jesus," was all Sean had time to say before the SUV ricocheted off Jordan's nearly buried Jeep into the wrought iron fence. With a squeal of twisted metal the Durango blasted through the gap. Jordan cut the wheel hard right and after a sickening moment of weightlessness, the Durango's tires dropped onto solid ground, found traction and tore forward through the snow down Mulberry Road toward town.

After a mile or so when Jordan's breathing started heading toward normal, he reached for his radio and tried to contact Kelly. After a few unsuccessful attempts, Jordan tossed the radio into the passenger seat.

"Anything yet?" Sean asked.

Jordan shook his head.

Sean looked to Bishop sitting beside him in the back seat. He hadn't said a word since leaving the Matthews' house. He silently reloaded his weapons.

"I have to get my son," Sean said.

Bishop met Sean's gaze for a moment and then went back to reloading his weapons.

CHAPTER 30

Ten minutes later the Durango pulled up in front of the Violet House, the engine making a grinding sound of metal on metal. All three of them spilled into the street and the blowing snow. Sean had torn some cloth to make a makeshift tourniquet for his hand and his leg, but neither cut was deep.

Bishop stared up at the dark building, studying.

"We go in, we search, then we leave," he said.

"You can leave right now if you want," Sean said and started toward the Violet House. "I'm not leaving without my son."

Like every other door on this street, they found the door to the Violet House smashed open, as was the front store window that faced the street. Sean felt sick as he stepped over broken glass and shattered wood. Together their flashlights swept over every inch of her place. They covered the downstairs quickly, finding nothing but damage.

Bishop and Jordan followed Sean up the stairs to Violet's apartment. They found the door lying in the hall. Deep claw marks crisscrossed the wood.

Inside the apartment candles burned, guttering in the wind. Sean moved to rush inside, but Bishop grabbed him and held him back. Sean wrestled out of his grip but made no move to go in.

"Kevin?" Sean cried. "Kevin?"

The first door on the left was closed but not locked. The heavily damaged door swung. Inside the tiny bathroom, blood was splashed across the ceramic floor. There were no bodies.

Sean felt hollowed out, gutted. His knees buckled and he dropped. He hit the ground hard at the edge of a puddle of blood and wept. After a moment, Bishop touched his shoulder, sending Sean springing to his feet.

"Don't touch me!" he screamed. "Get the fuck off me!"

Bishop backed up.

"Kevin! Kevin!" Sean screamed.

Bishop kept his eyes moving, scanning the dark apartment.

Sean spun and pointed at Bishop. "You did this!" Sean said. "You did this!"

"Sean," Bishop said.

"Go fuck yourself!"

"Sean, there are people in this town who still need you."

Sean was reeling now. He dropped down onto a sofa and let his gun fall to the floor.

"They took my son," he said. "Kevin!"

"I know."

"They took my son."

"Sean, listen to me," Bishop said.

"Where is he?" Sean asked. "Where is he? Tell me!"

"Sean," Bishop said, "Kevin is gone."

But Sean was already shaking his head.

"No, no, no," he whispered. "Where is he? Where did they take him?"

Jordan leaned out through the shattered window and scanned the street. He stumbled backwards into the apartment in a daze, clutching his neck. A claw had raked through the air and cut three grooves across his throat continuing down his chest to rip the front of his coat to shreds. Jordan reeled as Bishop fired at the windowsill where the Zijin reared its ugly head. The bullets ripped the top of its smooth head off and the creature fell limply into the street below.

Jordan touched the wound with freezing fingers and felt warm blood. He pressed his palm to the wound and felt his pulse pumping against his flesh.

Bishop scanned the area around the window. The dead Zijin lay still in the falling snow.

Jordan lay on the couch. His eyes were the only part of him moving, restlessly scanning the room. Bishop disappeared into the bathroom and returned with gauze, tape and a bottle of Tylenol. He dumped the items into Jordan's lap, jerking him out of his stupor.

"Wrap the wound," Bishop said. "Let's go."

Jordan pawed at the gauze.

"Can you walk?" asked Sean.

"Nothing wrong with my legs," Jordan said.

"Good. Get up," Bishop said.

After Jordan wrapped his wound and downed a handful of Tylenol, he got to his feet. Bishop tossed him a weapon and Jordan caught it out of the air.

"You're going to need that," he said. "Don't throw this one away.'

Sean led the three of them out of the Violet House into the street. It was cold inside the apartment, but outside was ridiculous. The wind snatched away his breath and froze his lungs with every inhalation. The small group trudged through the snow to the borrowed Durango where a small group of wraiths had crowded around the big SUV. Oliver was in front, waiting.

"It's not good, Bishop," Oliver said. "She's at St. Patrick's. She's in the bloody building."

Sean watched Bishop. He was staring at something near the Durango. His face fell.

"What is it?" Sean asked.

"Petra's at the church."

Jordan slid behind the wheel and turned the key. The engine whined and sputtered and finally died.

Sean was already looking around. Then he headed north on foot toward Cross Street, followed by Jordan. He made a sharp left down an alley between an electronics store called Spark and the town's only Laundromat. Bishop brought up the rear keeping watch.

Sean tried the door to Stan's Auto but found it locked. He broke the glass door with the butt of his pistol. No alarm sounded.

The sales office was dark but neat. Stan's Auto was closed early this time of year, thus no people, thus no damage by the Zijin. Sean moved to the pegboard in Stan's office and searched through the hanging keys.

Bishop waited in the showroom. There were four snowmobiles, an SUV and a quad on display. A few minutes later Sean emerged from the sales office and tossed Bishop a jumble of keys. He and Jordan fired up the snowmobiles.

"Jordan, you lead. Bishop, you go second, and I'll bring up the rear." Sean said. "Straight to the church."

Jordan nodded.

Sean fired three rounds into the main showroom window, shattering the glass.

Jordan tore out of the showroom into the snow, followed

by Bishop.

⁂

Sean tried to concentrate on the road but with near zero visibility he wasn't able to travel as fast as he would have liked. Two minutes in he could barely see Bishop's taillights. A moment later they were gone. Sean cursed under his breath and goosed the throttle. Over the wind and the drone of the snowmobile Sean heard three quick gunshots and his stomach turned over.

Was he the only one left alive out here?

He found Bishop's snowmobile a minute later. It was smashed into the grill of a parked car. Bishop was gone. Sean couldn't even hear Jordan's snowmobile anymore. He scanned the snow-swept street and saw only white.

"Bishop!" he cried, but the wind snatched away his call before it could get very far.

"Bishop!"

Sean drew his pistol and flashlight and scanned the area. He might as well have been on the moon. He was the only light for as far as he could see and that thought suddenly made him realize how very vulnerable he was right then.

Bishop was probably already beyond help, and if the creatures could get him, what chance did he have to save him? Or himself, for that matter? The flashlight felt more like a candle in the wind, his gun like a kid's toy. The wind and snow swirled around him, and the rapid chittering of the Zijin grew near. His pale face whipped left and right. He cranked the throttle and pulled quickly into the street.

CHAPTER 31

Norman fixed himself a cup of coffee and shuffled into the main reception area of the church where on Sundays after Mass the congregation gathered, drank coffee, nibbled on baked goods and talked about the weather and Osama bin Laden. Tonight's was an altogether different crowd. People from all over town were gathered in the tiny room, about sixty in all. For most of them, this was their first visit to the church since settling here in Danaid; for others it was as familiar as their own home. But the reception area had never looked like this. People lay on cots and sat in chairs, collapsed. Exhausted or wounded, they were spent.

Anyone who had any energy left was busy eating soup and sandwiches at a few tables set up near the kitchen. Others stared out into the darkness through the tiny slit windows. Nearly half were crying.

He found an empty seat at a table where Gertie sat quietly. The old girl toyed with a bowl of soup, not really eating. When Norman sat down, she nodded politely and went back to her stirring.

"Not hungry?" Norman asked.

Gertie shook her head. Her shoulders shook.

"Hey, hey, hey," Norman whispered, "it's okay."

She wiped tears off her cheeks and brushed back her hair.

"No, it's not okay." Gertie whispered. "Stupid old bat, leaking everywhere for all the world to see."

"It's all right," Norman replied. "It's only me."

"We're gonna die here, Norman" she said suddenly. "All of us."

Norman stared right back at her and didn't argue. The church was a trap. He realized that now. It had been a trap from the very start. But what else could they do? If they stayed in their houses they were taken. They couldn't leave Danaid, so here they were, trapped.

Gertie left the table and headed for the restroom. Norman watched her go without a word.

Eyes met his across the common area, the flat, cold eyes of a wraith. He looked around the room and saw more and more flooding into the common area, mixing with the living. Waiting. Watching. Something was about to happen. He sipped his coffee and kept his eyes on the table.

"You have to leave this place." Norman's mother whispered. "Right now."

She had taken a seat across from him as silently as a shadow. Her small round face was pinched with worry and concern. Norman shook his head slowly.

"I have nowhere to go."

Gertie pushed through the bathroom door and headed for the sinks. Her face was a mess. Her eyes were red and swollen while the rest of her face was a sickly gray. She ran the hot water and washed her hands. She cupped her hands together and splashed her face. The warm water felt wonderful. She blinked into the mirror and jumped as Petra appeared behind her. She tried to say something but it was cut short. Petra grabbed the back of Gertie's head and slammed it into the mirror. The mirror splintered and cracked and Gertie's nose spouted blood. Petra dropped the old woman to the floor in a heap and straddled her high on the back. Again and again she slammed Gertie's face against the tile floor.

Behind her, footsteps entered the bathroom and drew near. Slowly, Petra rose. Mabel and Sadie stood three feet away.

"Have the others arrived?" Petra asked.

"Yes, Lord," Mabel answered. "We are ready."

"By dawn there will not be a single human left in Danaid."

"Yes, Lord," Sadie and Mabel answered together.

"Not one. Even one could cause suspicion. Even one could cause doubt. The transition must be seamless."

"Yes, Lord."

Norman turned his attention to a young mother lying on one of the cots set up throughout the common area. She smoothed a small child's hair as he slept. He thought he might have seen her working in the town library, but he couldn't be sure. It didn't matter. Not now. Her lips moved silently and he knew that she was praying. He hoped it would help.

Darkness flooded the common area as the power was cut. Screams erupted all around him. Norman couldn't move, he was welded to his seat. He saw movement through the blackness. He could hear the panting breath he wished to God he would never have to hear again, and then he was ripped out of his seat, high up into the air. Sharp talons ripped into the flesh around his neck and he struggled to breathe. His legs and arms flailed and kicked, but it was no use. The arms that held him were made of iron. His body was slammed down into the floor and what little breath he did possess rushed from him in an instant. He could barely hear the crying and screaming all around him for the sound of his heart in his ears. He saw a face swim into his line of sight. A face he knew. A face he once followed and photographed.

"You will be beautiful," Petra whispered.

Norman felt pressure across his throat and then nothing but darkness.

A Zijin clambered onto a parked car up ahead. Sean gave the sled more gas but the scrabbling footsteps of the Zijin grew louder. The creature ran along the line of parked cars to his right, or his left, or both. He couldn't even look to be sure. His eyes were pinned to the road. The sound seemed to come from everywhere in the swirling wind. He would have prayed but he was too scared and he didn't have the breath to spare anyway.

Behind him he heard the Zijin's strange language, the frenzied animal panting of their breath. He gunned the throttle and the machine lurched forward. He drove as fast as he could see, and then some. The lone headlight pushed the darkness and the storm away ten feet at a time. By the time he saw them standing there, waiting, it was too late to do anything but go faster. He broke through the gauntlet, the wall of four waiting Zijin. Their claws like razors tore through his jacket. Pain ripped through his right shoulder and spread through his chest like a brush fire. Out of the dark what felt like a club bludgeoned him across the temple. He slumped in his seat as his head was forced to the steering wheel. His vision swam and his hand slipped off the accelerator, but he managed to stay seated. He was still conscious with only one thought—Kevin. For if he fell now, or even slowed down, he was dead for sure. His hand curled over the accelerator and the sled cut down the street.

CHAPTER 32

The crushing weight of the creature ripped Bishop from the seat of his sled to the ground where they landed hard, plowing through the deep snow. Bishop tried to get up but was immediately slammed back down and pinned. His blade slid into his right hand and by bending his wrist to its fullest extent he was able to wound the thing. The Zijin spun away from the blade, allowing Bishop to snap to his feet and pull his gun. The second Zijin leapt from a parked car and caught three bullets in the chest, spinning the creature like a top in a flurry of sparks. The Zijin that had pinned him leapt onto his back and forced Bishop to the ground, knocking the gun from his hand. Bishop rolled out of the creature's grip and drove all seven inches of his black blade up under the creature's chin. It died shuddering in the snow.

Bishop rose to his feet and searched for his fallen weapon. His hands brushed through the nearest drifts of snow without finding it. There was no time. Claws scraped across metal nearby as more Zijin closed in on him. With the sled down and out, he cut through an alley between the pub and the café and moved in the general direction of the church. It was still a good mile away, but he'd be lucky to make it another ten feet on foot.

He stayed close to the tree cover and then dashed to the nearest house, a tiny, dark brick dwelling set back from the road. Bishop was closest to the side door and found it locked. The lock was easy enough to pick, and he was inside in under a minute. He locked and bolted the door behind him and listened to the darkness.

He found himself in a small kitchen. Baskets of plastic fruit were left on the kitchen table. The large fridge was plastered with pictures of people of all ages. Kids, middle aged, elderly, all smiled into the camera. Bishop wondered how many of them were still alive.

He peered out through the thin curtains that hung over the kitchen sink and saw a crowd of Zijin in front of the little house, waiting for a sign, a signal as to his whereabouts. Their heads whipped left and right searching for him.

The ground floor was dark. He had lost his flashlight so he moved slowly, feeling his way through the dining room furniture toward a basement door. The door was ajar. Bishop stepped through and descended the stairs. At the bottom of the stairs, in the center of the floor was a flashlight.

He was halfway down when a voice said, "Hello?"

He stopped.

The word was right but the voice wasn't.

"Hello?"

The voice sounded wrong, almost mechanical. Bishop held his breath. The handle of his hidden dagger slid into his waiting palm as he took another step down to the next riser.

"Hello," the voice pleaded. Sounding better but still warbled, like the person was talking through water.

Bishop reached the end of the stairs and stepped into the weak beam of the flashlight.

"Hello," the boy's voice whispered. "Help me." The boy stood ten feet from him. He was naked. His pale skin looked ashen in the flickering light. The skin of the boy's chest rippled and bulged, twisting off his body as something pressed against it, fighting to get out.

Bishop snatched up the flashlight and scanned the room. The basement was packed, wall to wall with the hapless inhabitants of the house. The naked family lay on their backs, trembling, as the transformation process ran its course. Their skin was already falling away. Their chests heaved with rapid, animal panting.

"Hello," the boy said, "Bishop."

He saw not the boy but his daughter, Eve. She crouched in the weak light at the head of her mother, who lay prone on the floor. He saw Eve's eyes, and the way they shone that night, her beautiful face curled in a sneer of contempt and rage. The boy turned and the skin of his face cracked and fell away.

The boy made a loud, shrill call. His eyes flashed on Bishop and he charged, mouth open, arms outstretched.

Bishop threw the knife without thinking. In one swift movement, the knife cut through the air and entered the boy's forehead. The creature stumbled and dropped to the floor.

Suddenly the basement windows exploded inward as the Zijin flooded inside. They swarmed Bishop from all sides and blocked his one exit. They fell upon him like a gray shuddering mass, biting and snarling, clawing and scratching. Bishop's blood splashed over the concrete floor. He screamed a short, angry roar. From within his coat Bishop drew another edged weapon and killed the Zijin to his immediate right.

Another creature knocked the flashlight from Bishop's hand and dropped the basement into total darkness. Bishop smiled and flew into the crowd of Zijin like a hurricane.

✤

Jordan didn't see anything around him and he didn't hear anything, and that's exactly what he wanted. He just wanted to get to the church. With Petra at the church, his plan was to wait for Sean and Bishop to show up. Jordan was a lot of things, but a hero he was not. It's not that he wasn't brave. It was just that he didn't want to die. And until today he hadn't fired his weapon at a single living thing.

Things were moving too fast. He thought of his old life, wearing the badge and cruising the town, maybe breaking up a domestic or two on the weekends, and it felt unreal to him now. His world had changed and he had no choice but to change with it.

He was within sight of the church when the front doors burst open and two people in shirtsleeves ran down the stairs screaming. He swerved the snowmobile behind a parked car and killed the engine.

The two people were Hillary Kilroy who owned the flower shop on Cross St. and Steve Poole. They were both in their fifties and it looked like the last time they had run was in high school. But they were running now, arms pumping, bellies swinging from side to side. Hillary stole a look over her shoulder and slipped on the icy street. She screamed and fell in a heap into the snow. She looked to Steve but he hadn't even slowed.

Jordan reached for his gun, but he was too far away to even think about hitting anything. He took a few steps up the street, staying low, and then he froze. Three Zijin leapt from the front entrance of the church and down the stairs in a single bound. They roared and charged after the two escapees.

Hillary was halfway to her feet when she was drilled to the ground by one of them. She was flipped onto her back and pummeled by the huge fists of the creature. When she stopped struggling the Zijin scooped the heavy woman onto its shoulder as if she weighed less than a sack of potatoes and carried her quickly back inside the church.

The other two were busy with Steve. He didn't look like he was built for speed, but fear and adrenaline can do wonders for some people. Steve never looked back. He ran hard and straight and was about fifty feet from Jordan when he was finally overtaken.

Jordan saw the fear in Steve's face, the look in his eyes, and then the desperation when their eyes met. Steve opened his mouth to scream or beg Jordan for help, but whatever it was, it was cut short as one of the Zijin bit into the side of Steve's throat. Hot red blood exploded into the snow. Steve spasmed for a moment, and then lay still. The pair of Zijin hoisted him and spirited him away.

Jordan dropped down behind the parked car tasting vomit in the back of his throat. He shook so bad he couldn't hold his weapon. It dropped soundlessly between his legs. He sat there for a long time, too scared to move or even breathe. He was getting colder and he knew he had to warn the others.

The low drone of a snowmobile approached. He clutched his weapon like a talisman close to his chest and slowly, carefully rolled to his knees and peered out into the street. When he saw Sean barreling up the street he aimed his flashlight at him and flicked it on and off until Sean swerved and headed toward his position.

Bishop shuffled through the shadows looking like he had walked through Hell. His face was splashed with blood. Some of it was his. Wounds, still fresh, trickled blood down his sleeves and over his back. His head felt like it had been squeezed in a vise. He passed a row of evergreens and saw that the church was dark and cold. No lights burned over the front entrance. The basement windows were black. He was too late.

Oliver Dannon sat on the front steps waiting for him. He shook his head.

"They're all gone, lad," he said.

Bishop struggled toward Oliver and dropped onto a step beside him. He didn't say a word, just concentrated on his breathing. In and out. Slow and easy. There were still ragged holes in his chest and lungs and he wheezed with the effort.

"Are you all right? Did you hear what I said?"

"I heard you," Bishop gasped. "Where did they go?"

"They've gone to the nest, boy," Oliver replied. "In the mine."

"Is she there?"

Oliver nodded. "At least for the moment."

"Is anyone else left?"

"Sean Berlin and the deputy, Jordan Hanson are at the Trading Post."

CHAPTER 33

Sean sat in Billy Walter's old chair in the small office of the Trading Post. He laced up new, dry boots and felt every muscle pull and ache as he bent over to set the knot. When he was finished, he straightened and a sharp pain like a quick jab to his chest took his breath away. For a moment he couldn't breathe. When his breath returned it came in gasps. He coughed and tasted blood. He wiped his mouth clean with the back of his hand and rose to his feet.

He closed his eyes and tried to think of Petra and Kevin, the way they were, warm and safe, watching movies together on the couch as the snow pounded down outside. But it didn't work. The storm was there, and so was the snow, but he couldn't remember any good times now. When he thought of Petra and Kevin, he saw them screaming. He saw monsters gliding through the shadows, reaching out, ripping away.

He opened his eyes.

Sean slipped his arms into the sleeves of his coat, turned around, and found Bishop Kane standing in the doorway. He hadn't heard so much as a footstep. Sean dropped back into Billy's old chair and asked, "Got a cigarette?"

Bishop rummaged through a coat pocket and came up with a crumpled pack. He tossed them to Sean. He lit one and drew deeply.

"I came here for one reason, Sean," Bishop began, "and that hasn't changed."

"You came to kill Petra."

"You should know," Bishop said, "Petra was more than she seemed."

Sean stared hard at Bishop, almost begging him to smear her name, to give him any excuse to jump across the short distance between them.

"I lived here once. Did you know that? Back in '76," Bishop said. "I was a carpenter, contractor. I had a wife, a house, and a little daughter. Eve.

"She was very sick. Slept all the time..Doctors didn't have a clue, so they told us it was a million different things. We took her as far as California for treatment. Nothing worked. No matter what we did, she got worse. She slept more, and that wouldn't have been so bad, except for the nightmares. She'd wake up out of a dead sleep, screaming, thrashing, wailing. My wife and I, I bet you, we didn't get three solid hours of sleep a night for three months.

"In the end we decided to take care of her ourselves. I got a second job and my wife quit hers so she could tend to Eve."

Bishop pulled the cigarette from his mouth and crushed it under his boot.

November 13, 1976

Bishop slipped inside out of the wind and the rain and eased the door shut. He stripped off his soaked jacket and hung it on a hook next to his wife's navy windbreaker. It was late and he assumed that his wife would be in bed by now, but he could hear the television in the sunroom.

"Sara?" he said. "You still up?"

Bishop kicked off his boots and stepped up into the kitchen.

He snagged a beer from the fridge, twisted off the cap and slugged back most of the bottle. He did the slow walk through the kitchen, fingering the mail, more bills as usual, opened the newspaper to the sports page, sighed and continued into the sunroom.

The television was on, but the room was empty. Odd, he thought. Why wouldn't Sara turn off the television if she was going to bed? Bishop shrugged. He was too tired. As was probably the case with Sara. He imagined her watching the tube and then hearing one of Eve's nightly screams for help as she struggled with yet another nightmare.

He turned off the living room lamps as he made his way to the stairs. He stopped at the front door and peered out into the dark, rain-slick street. No one out at this time of night, just leaves skating across the tarmac. He climbed the carpeted stairs wearily, realizing just how bone tired he was. For the last three months he hadn't got much sleep, and it was taking its toll on both him and his wife. Conversation dwindled, as did the affection between them. They were drifting apart. In the beginning they had only one prayer, and that was for their daughter to get well both mentally and physically, but now they added a second wish to their prayers; they prayed that somehow they could get their life back, the way it used to be. They prayed that they could one day smile without flinching.

Bishop reached the top of the stairs and after a quick stop in the bathroom, he stopped by the first door on his right. In the past he had always enjoyed peeking in on his daughter. He loved the way the room smelled like a child slept there. Little girl dolls, plush toys, even the soft blankets all brought a smile to his weary face as he stepped inside. But there was no one there, no one sleeping in the bed.

Bishop hurried to the master bedroom. The room was dark and quiet. Pale yellow light from the street lamps outside filtered in through the blinds. The flannel sheets that Sara loved so much were pushed into a heap at the foot of the empty bed.

"Sara?"

Bishop turned in place, a little confused. He took a quick peek around the bed, found the floor empty and retraced his steps back down the hall to the top of the stairs.

"Sara?" He waited, hand on the banister, and listened to the wind outside push against the house, causing it to shift and groan.

"Eve?"

A crash and the tinkling of falling metal came from the kitchen. He cursed under his breath and padded down the stairs. Bishop's heart was in his throat, his stomach tightened. Jesus Christ, he thought, what now?

When he stepped into the kitchen he stopped cold. Scattered across the floor were the contents of a drawer. Spoons, forks and knives glittered in the weak light. Standing amid the scattered silverware he called to each of them again. Not even the wind answered this time. He was about to call out again when a sound stopped him, low and muffled. Whispering? Who was whispering?

Bishop inched closer to the basement stairs. There was nothing at first, then he heard it again. Soft and low, he couldn't make it out, but someone was whispering in the basement.

He took the creaking wooden stairs slowly to the bottom and snapped on the wall switch.

The bare sixty-watt bulb that hung from the ceiling sparked

to life and cast shadows from the washer and dryer, the battered laundry basket piled high with dirty clothes, and the boxes of detergent and dryer sheets that sat to one side of the wobbly metal table.

"Sara? Eve? Are you down here?" he asked, as he moved slowly through the basement.

After they had moved in, Sara had installed, instead of a door, a curtain that separated the main basement from the room she called the "junk drawer." The curtain was greenish brown and covered in a smattering of orange and blue flowers. It was hideous, but she loved it and that was enough for him.

The whispering continued, clearly now, the words came fast in a steady stream. They sounded foreign. For the first time since arriving home and finding his wife and daughter missing, Bishop was nervous. He stopped in his tracks and looked around for a weapon. His golf clubs were the first thing he spotted. He pulled the putter out of the bag and gripped it like a baseball bat, already feeling silly.

At the curtain he stopped. The voice behind it was not one he was used to. It sounded older, deeper. His hand reached for the curtain and as his fingers touched the cloth the whispering was cut short. Silence flooded in. A deep chill ran through him. Bishop checked his grip on the putter, grabbed the curtain and yanked it back.

The junk drawer was filled with boxes and odds and ends accumulated over years of living with a packrat. His wife was infamous for saving, packing and storing useless or broken items, like legs to a table they no longer owned, or old calendars.

Boxes were stacked to the ceiling, filled with unsorted

pictures that were supposed to make it into an album one day. Christmas decorations that never made it up to the main floor anymore dominated one corner, and along the right hand wall a paint-splattered shelf stretched the length of the room where half-used cans of paint, varsol, paint thinner, rollers and trays, new and old, sat waiting for their next project.

Bishop found them in the center of the room and the sight took his breath away, like a physical blow. He couldn't move or speak, and it felt as if his heart would burst through his ribcage.

His wife had been stripped naked. She lay prone on the bare concrete floor. His daughter Eve, in her nightgown, stood over her. His eyes were riveted to his wife. Her beautiful green eyes stared straight at the ceiling, unblinking. Her chest rose and fell quickly. Her pale skin looked almost gray. Strange characters and symbols seemed branded on her skin, but the brands looked as though they were rising up through her skin, pushing against her flesh. Sara's breathing quickened until she was nearly panting. The putter slipped through Bishop's fingers to the floor.

Eve stared at her father through the sweaty tangles of her dark hair. Her body was still. The very air around her seemed to tremble.

"What happened?" Bishop whispered breathlessly. "What did you do?"

For a moment Eve didn't speak. A small smile curled her lips up at the corners. The same markings that marred his wife's body traced their way over her ivory skin. Delicate and intricate, the writing wrapped around her limbs like the thin tendrils of a living thing. And when she spoke, it was not her voice, not the voice of a ten-year-old girl, but of a nation. A nation of hate. A nation of power, speaking as one.

"This is only the beginning," she whispered. "She is the first."

"Oh, Jesus Christ, Eve, please."

Bishop felt like he was drowning right there in his basement. He wanted to say something, anything, but his throat was filled with sand.

In her right hand, Eve held the handle of a filleting knife. Its thin blade winked menacingly in the weak light.

For a moment, a mere flash, he thought he saw his daughter standing there, his Eve, his little angel. Alone. Afraid.

"I can hear them ... screaming," she whispered.

Bishop took a half step toward her and she sliced the air between them, freezing him in place.

"Eve, please," he pleaded.

Bishop advanced again and reached out for her, but Eve's movements were fluid, quick and sure. She sidestepped her father's advance and shot out her right arm. Her blade flashed before she buried it in her father. Bishop screamed and twisted away, but she held him close, driving the blade up and back through his stomach until the blade struck the bone of his ribcage. Bishop yanked himself from her grip and fell backwards into a stack of boxes before falling awkwardly to the floor where hundreds of snapshots spilled from the broken crates.

Eve turned away and stepped toward the long wall of painting supplies. She stood at the shelf and ran the fingers of her left hand over the labels. Her fingers trailed over the robin's egg blue that her mother had painted the sunroom, the rose of the living room, and the countless cans of white.

On the floor, Bishop's wife was frozen in place, her gray skin taut with the markings that threatened to rip through her. Suddenly, she stopped panting and grew still.

Eve selected a can, pulled it from the shelf and placed it at her feet. With the tip of her knife she pried off the lid.

"Eve. Please. Stop." Bishop begged from where he lay. He pressed his hand to his wound, but he could not stop the bleeding. It flowed through his fingers, pooling beneath him. If Eve heard, she gave no notice. The lid came off and she set it down neatly beside the can.

Bishop fought against the bright sparks of pain that shot through his side as he dragged himself to his feet.

"Eve," he said. There was no response as she lifted the can of paint thinner off the ground.

"Eve! Look at me!" he barked.

Eve's eyes snapped up and bore straight through him. Her black hair hung in thick tangles, framing her thin white face. Bishop thought she looked stripped, like a car built for speed, reduced to only a tank of gas and a seat, a machine built for a single purpose.

But for a moment, a flicker that could have been a trick of the light, he saw the girl he once knew, just beneath the surface, as if she struggled for control inside her own body. Her eyes were red and swollen with tears.

"Run," she begged.

Suddenly, Sara dug her fingernails into the concrete, snapping them off and sending them skittering across the floor. Her back arched and she screamed.

"Oh, Jesus God," was all Bishop could muster. "Oh, God,

Eve."

"Run …" Eve said as she lifted the can of paint thinner over her head.

Sara's skin split down the middle with the sound of ripping leather, revealing a gray-skinned body crisscrossed with a network of black veins. Her muscles stretched and grew, lining her expanding frame as her mouth snapped shut crushing her old teeth to reveal a new set of razor sharp replacements.

"Run, daddy," Eve begged, her voice thick with desperation.

Bishop couldn't take his eyes off Sara, or the creature that she had become. The creature's head snapped to the right and its black eyes found Bishop.

"Go!" Eve screamed.

Eve splashed the can's contents around the room, coating boxes and bolts of material and letting the remainder pool at her feet, soaking the hem of her nightgown. In her right hand she held a Zippo.

The creature leapt into a crouch behind her, waiting.

Eve spun the wheel and opened the flame. She held the lighter for a moment, calmly letting the flame dance in front of her eyes. And then she let it fall.

The creature leapt across the gap for Bishop, but he was already gone.

Bishop tore through the curtain that hung in the doorway and raced to the stairs. The creature charged at him from behind, but he didn't dare look back. He was bleeding badly, but at that moment his body ran on fear. He topped the risers, slipped into the kitchen and locked the door behind him.

Sean watched him. His cigarette was long gone.

"So what happened?" he asked.

"I turned on the gas stove and waited."

"You blew up your house?"

Bishop nodded.

"Killed your wife and your daughter."

"No," Bishop replied. "Eve killed my wife. Or rather, what was inside Eve killed her. Eve didn't die."

"So …"

"Petra is Eve," Bishop said. "Petra, or whatever the hell she's calling herself these days, is my daughter. After I died, it turned out that I was rather special, in that I had a choice. Rot in the earth for all eternity, or—"

"Hunt monsters?"

"I work for an organization called the Ministry of the Wraith. They use wraiths to find … undesirables that have found their way into our world. Once the wraiths find the target, a hunter is dispatched to eliminate them."

"If this is true—"

"Sean, you've seen them," Bishop said. "You know it's true."

"So what is she?" he asked. "What is inside her?"

"The Ministry calls Eve an 'open door,' a kind of conduit between worlds. Eve was that portal for a race called the Zijin. It was as if the entire race had been downloaded into her DNA. Don't ask me how. As soon as she was ready, physically, she began to reproduce the Zijin race through humans, starting with my wife."

"How?"

"The writing on the floor, the language is Zijin. The Ministry calls it the Blood Figure. She has been doing this undetected for nearly thirty years. She moves from town to town infecting those she can use. They in turn infect others. The best part is that when they aren't hunting, like they are now, they look just like you and me. They hold down jobs, drive your kids to school, serve your food. They are everywhere. Hiding in plain sight. Invisible. And their numbers are growing every day."

Sean closed his eyes. This wasn't happening. It couldn't be. A world beneath the one he knew? It was impossible. Except, he had seen them, these Zijin. He had fought them. They were real. Real enough to kill. He believed. Everything. There were ghosts all around. Wraiths. Watching, silently. The dark was filled with gliding monsters that looked to feed and reproduce their race.

Sean opened his eyes. Jordan had found his way into his room. He looked scared and sick, and Sean knew that he had heard Bishop's story.

"How long?" Sean asked.

"How long for what?"

"How long until Kevin …" he stopped. "Until Kevin is one of those things? A Zijin?"

Bishop turned and faced Sean.

"Kevin is gone, Sean."

"No. There has to be a chance."

"There's always a chance, but—"

"Then there's a chance he's still alive."

Bishop nodded grudgingly. "There's a chance, but you have to remember what we're doing here. Look at all the people you lost tonight. This town is gone. Tomorrow when the sun comes up the people that will run the shops and look like your friends, won't be. They won't even be human. They will be the Zijin. We cannot allow that to happen. Cut off the head and the body dies. Killing Petra is our purpose. That is our mission. Do you understand?"

Sean nodded.

"She's at the mine," Bishop said.

Sean looked him in the eye. "Let's do it."

CHAPTER 34

Jordan carried three lightweight backpacks out the back door of the Trading Post to where Sean and Bishop stood in front of a line of snowmobiles. He handed out the packs and the three men climbed aboard their sleds and fired up the engines.

It took about twenty minutes to reach the edge of the clearing near the Monk's Head Mine. The three men climbed off their snowmobiles and drew their weapons. It was dawn, or thereabouts. The sky was the color of a bad bruise, all purples and black, and the snow wasn't letting up. It came from all angles, erasing their footsteps as fast as they made them.

Bishop scanned the mine and the surrounding area from the edge of the clearing. He couldn't see much of the structure but he didn't have to. Hundreds of wraiths surrounded the building from about fifty feet out. Their forms shuddered and blurred in the wind and snow, but their eyes were constant. Some stared at the building hidden behind the storm, but most stared at him.

For a long time after becoming a hunter, Bishop had thought that he was unnatural, a freak, something that shouldn't be. But lately, especially now, when his mind wandered toward the philosophical nature of being, he wondered if it was his first life, his "normal" life, that had been a freak, a dream. It didn't matter. What was happening now, in the present, was all that mattered. Death is a door. He had heard that phrase enough in the Ministry from other hunters and wraiths all around the world that it might as well have been the Ministry of the Wraith's slogan. Death is a door to another room of your life.

He knew there was a very high probability that in the next few hours he could die, or be destroyed, whatever you wanted to call it. If death was a door, he wondered where the next door would take him, if indeed there was another door. For the first time in a long time, he felt afraid.

After a quick discussion about how to get in without being seen by the Zijin guarding the mine, Sean and Bishop followed Jordan through a stand of trees, and down a small slope to a nearly snow-covered sewer grate.

"A tunnel?" Sean asked.

"It's our best shot," Jordan replied.

The trio entered the tunnel and their flashlights sparked to life, playing over the curved steel walls and ceiling. Every sound echoed until they sounded like a shuffling herd of elephants. As they moved deeper into the tunnel what little sunlight there was disappeared behind them. When the tunnel veered to the right, it sealed the three men in darkness.

Ten minutes in, Jordan stopped and leaned against the wall, out of breath. They had to hunch over to keep their packs from dragging against the ceiling and the sides of the tunnel, and that put strain on their lower backs and their knees. They were all appreciative of the break.

"Where does this lead?" asked Sean.

"It runs right under the administration part of the building to the mine," Jordan replied.

Bishop took a few steps and swept his light across another

tunnel that branched off their own. His beam illuminated dripping water and an empty tunnel. No Zijin. Bishop waited for a moment and listened. After a long last look, he spun in place and trudged back to Sean and Jordan.

Jordan moved faster now, making quick lefts and rights through the maze of the sewer system. The trio moved at a near jog when Sean stopped suddenly and caused Bishop to pile into him from behind.

"What is it?" Bishop asked.

"Listen," Sean whispered.

Water dripped all around and their breathing was harsh and tinny, but there was something else. Sean turned and swept his light behind them. Bishop lent his light to the cause and together they lit the entire width of the tunnel. Twenty yards back, Sean saw something, a tiny cloud of steam, a tiny cloud of breath. He waited, rooted to his spot until his light lit the face of a Zijin as it peered around the corner.

"Run!" Sean shouted.

Bishop grabbed Jordan and pushed him forward. Sean pulled his gun and fired down the tunnel. Bishop slipped in front of Sean, putting himself between the Zijin and his partners.

"Go," he said. "Don't wait for me."

Sean turned and disappeared as he chased after Jordan.

With one hand Bishop laid down a suppressing fire and with the other he dug into his coat pocket. He placed the small object he retrieved from his pocket against the tunnel wall. It was the size and color of a hockey puck. Then he moved, double-timing it backwards, reloading his weapon. His flashlight swept back and forth, flashing over the charging Zijin as they flooded through the tunnel, rippled with muscle and screaming for blood.

Bishop fired a few more shots into the rushing crowd and then turned and ran. In his hand he held a small remote control device. Until he was tackled and the remote was knocked away. Suddenly Bishop was on his back, pinned. His light lay broken and useless in the six inches of water that covered the floor. Bishop couldn't see the creature, but he could feel its talons digging into the flesh of his shoulders, he could feel the monster's rancid breath on his throat.

Further down the tunnel, Jordan slid to a stop under a grate. His flashlight swept over the grill and the surrounding area.

"This is it." Jordan said. "The access grate I told you about."

"Okay, let's go. Let's go!"

Jordan leapt up onto the grate and pulled. He hung from the metal grate, but it didn't budge. Jordan dropped down into the dark water.

"Fuck!" he spat. "It must be rusted tight. We're fucked. This tunnel ends about a hundred yards up ahead."

Sean pocketed his weapon, jumped up and grabbed the bars of the grate. He pulled his head close to the metal frame.

"It's padlocked," he said. "From the inside."

A scream, human or otherwise, ripped through the darkness. Sean leapt up onto the grate once again and drew his weapon. Jordan whispered, "Oh, shit," and took a few steps back.

"Look away," Sean said and fired.

Bishop bent his right wrist and the concealed, spring-loaded blade sprung from his sleeve straight through the Zijin's throat.

The Zijin reeled backwards clutching at its windpipe as Bishop rolled to his feet and decapitated the creature with a single swipe. He searched wildly for the remote control as the sound of chittering and scratching talons drew near.

Sean fired again and again and then crashed to the ground in a heap. Jordan was quick to his side and pulled him to his feet.

"Jesus Christ! Are you all right?"

Sean nodded and leapt up onto the grate. The lock had been obliterated. He yanked on the grill and it dropped a quarter of an inch. He yanked down again and the grill dropped three inches more.

Then they heard it.

A rolling thunder shook the tunnel, nearly sending Jordan to his knees, followed by the orange-red light of flame.

Sean yanked again and again on the grate as Jordan stared wide-eyed at the wave of flame that charged toward them.

"Jordan! Help me!" Sean screamed.

Jordan jumped onto the grate bars and applied all his weight to bring it down.

"C'mon, c'mon, c'mon," Sean whispered.

Finally, the grate swung open and both men dropped to the floor. They scrambled to their feet and Sean nearly threw Jordan up through the gap.

A wave of fire rushed toward Sean. He jumped and grabbed the grate then took Jordan's outstretched arm. He slithered through the gap and crawled head first into the dark. They scurried away from the grate seconds before a column of flame shot straight up from the hole in the floor.

Sean and Jordan stared at each other for a long moment.

"You okay?" Sean asked.

"No. Not at all, really."

Sean squeezed Jordan's shoulder.

"You're okay."

It took them a moment to regain their bearings, to find their flashlights, switch them on and scan the room. They were in a small room with a lot of empty metal shelving attached to the walls.

The sound of shuffling feet and movement below in the tunnel brought them back to the opening. Sean and Jordan aimed their flashlight beams and their weapons at the hole in the floor. They tensed as hands curled over the edge. With their fingers on their triggers, they watched Bishop calmly pull himself up into the empty room, looking ashen as always. He scanned the weary men as they let out a long sigh of relief and lowered their weapons to the floor.

"Good," Bishop said, "you're not dead."

Sean and Jordan nodded numbly.

"Then let's go."

CHAPTER 35

Jordan lead them out of the storeroom and, after taking a quick look down the hall in both directions, they slipped through a door marked RESTRICTED ACCESS into one of the mine's rock tunnels.

Here at least the ceiling was higher than in the sewer, which was both good and bad. Good because they were no longer forced to hunch over and thus had a wider range of motion, but bad because the Zijin had a penchant for clinging to high ceilings. Sean's light constantly scanned the ceiling and the surrounding area while Jordan's light was pinned to the floor as he searched for sinkholes and debris, among other things.

"How much further is it?" Sean asked.

"We're close to the bottom here," Jordan replied. "They hit water about twenty feet below us. I figure they're probably in the main auditorium. It's the biggest room down here. I'm taking us around behind it. Hopefully, they'll be surprised, give us more of a chance."

Jordan stopped dead.

"What?" Sean asked.

Sean moved to Bishop's right and swept his light over the tunnel ahead. The rock floor had apparently given way and was covered with a network of planks. The boards didn't look like they'd hold the weight of their flashlights let alone them.

"Is there another way?" Sean asked.

"No," Jordan replied.

"And even if there is," Bishop said, "we don't have time."

They had to keep going.

Jordan studied the boards with his light. Finally, he nodded.

"Are you sure?" Sean asked him.

"What choice do we have?" Jordan replied, "We'll go one at a time." Sean pushed to the front of the line and took the first step onto the planks.

He was five feet out on the wood floor when he knew it was a terrible mistake. The floor swayed under his weight and trembled with every step. He moved very slowly, inching along. The boards cracked and groaned. A cold sheet of sweat popped out over his skin. He froze and waited for the whole thing to collapse beneath him. But after the moment passed and the structure didn't collapse, Sean took another breath and started moving again.

Up ahead, the planks ended and solid rock returned. He stepped off the planks and breathed a little easier. Next Bishop passed over the boards and finally Jordan.

All eyes were on Jordan as he shuffle-stepped his way over the creaking boards. He looked scared and young and helpless as a crack ripped through the board between his feet.

"Run Jordan!" Sean shouted. "Run!"

But Jordan was pinned in place, afraid to move. Another crack like a lightning strike erupted until the sound of cracking wood seemed to come from everywhere.

Jordan's lower body disappeared. He threw out his arms and clung to the board he had, until recently, been standing on. He tried to pull himself up, but it was cracking, breaking away. He climbed hand over hand. He was ten feet away from solid ground.

Sean stopped and aimed his light back toward Jordan then raced back out onto the planks.

"Sean! No!" Bishop said.

Jordan looked up in time to see Sean racing over the boards.

"Sean!" was all Jordan had time to say before the board he had clung to snapped and Jordan dropped into the darkness.

"Jordan!" Sean screamed. He crawled to the edge of the hole and shone his light down into the depths.

"Jordan!"

Jordan fell hard into the wet rock floor. Something cracked in his leg and he squealed with pain.

About twenty feet down, Jordan found himself sitting in two feet of water. His body ached, but nothing hurt more than his right leg, just below the knee. He probed the darkness with his flashlight and took stock of his new surroundings. High up above he spotted Sean's light and gave him a little wave.

"You all right?" Sean asked.

"Just fucking wonderful," Jordan whispered to himself. "Yes! I'm alive," he called up to Sean. Jordan put his hands down to push himself up into a sitting position and screamed out.

"Fuck!"

Sean was right back at the hole shining his light down into the depths.

"What is it?"

Jordan ran his hand down his leg and found it. His right knee was facing ninety degrees the wrong way.

"It's my knee."

"Can you walk?" Sean asked.

Jordan tried to stand, or even roll to a crawling position but any movement brought excruciating pain. He cursed and swore and then flopped back down onto his back in the water.

"No."

"C'mon, what do you mean, no."

"I mean no. No, I can't walk, I can hardly move."

"Okay, hold on, we're gonna rig something up and get you out of there," Sean said. "Just sit tight."

"Was that a joke?"

"Just sit there, relax, we'll get you out."

Sean's light disappeared from the lip of the hole and Jordan suddenly felt completely alone.

Sean crawled away from the hole and pulled rope out of his pack. Bishop stood very still, scanning the tunnel walls.

"Pull the rope out of your pack, we might need it," Sean said.

"Sean, we don't have time for this," Bishop replied.

"We're gonna make time," Sean said. "We're not leaving him down there."

"Even if we get him up here we can't take him with us, and we can't leave him. He's as good down there as anywhere."

Sean pulled the rest of his rope out of his backpack and tied a harness.

"I'm not leaving him," Sean said. "You can help me, or you can stand there, but I'm not leaving him behind. No one else is gonna die today. Now gimme your fucking rope and help me pull him up."

Bishop shook his head and scanned the darkness, "Stubborn son of a bitch."

Sean lowered the harness as Bishop focused the beam of his flashlight down into the hole. Jordan yanked on the rope when he was ready.

"Okay, hold on!" Sean said.

Hand over hand they slowly brought Jordan toward the surface.

Jordan held a flashlight in his left hand and a pistol in his right. As he rose he scanned the crevasse. Tiny veins of water sluiced down over the rock walls. Long scratch marks scarred the rock. Jordan stopped breathing. He spun gently, but he craned his neck and twisted his arms to keep his light on the scratch marks. They were everywhere.

Jordan looked up to the mouth of the hole and it seemed a million miles away, as if he were being slowly pulled to the moon. He squeezed the pistol in his hand and took a few deep breaths. He was seven feet off the ground.

The chittering came first, and it was as if someone had thrown ice water on his heart. Everything stopped. Jordan spun toward the sound of running footsteps rushing out of the darkness. He brought up his light and illuminated the Zijin as it leapt toward him. Jordan screamed and fired.

The creature took three shots in the chest and kept coming. It leapt off the floor and slammed into Jordan. As they plunged back into the pit, it wrapped its arms around him and squeezed. Its smooth head darted toward Jordan and it drove its fangs into his left forearm. The creature's razor sharp teeth tore easily through Jordan's coat and skin. His sleeve filled up with blood as the bones in his arm were ground together between the creature's teeth.

"Jordan!" Sean screamed.

Jordan landed on top of the Zijin. With his free hand he fired and fired at close range, pressing the barrel of his weapon to the creature's head. Black blood of the Zijin splashed over his face and into his mouth but he couldn't stop firing. The Zijin whimpered and slowly its grip on Jordan loosened.

Jordan couldn't catch his breath. Everything hurt, including his knee, but he was standing. Standing on his good leg in the water and shaking violently.

"Jordan?" Sean asked.

"Get me the fuck out of here!"

Sean and Bishop got to their feet and worked faster, hand over hand. Jordan tried to reload his weapon, but his hands shook and he dropped the fresh clip into the water. He cursed and tried not to scream.

At his feet the dead Zijin's head looked like a pumpkin that had been dropped from a roof.

But there was more than one.

All around him was the drumming of feet and the scratching of claws and that horrible sound they made.

"Faster. Please. Faster guys!" Jordan whispered. "They're coming!"

Jordan searched his pockets for another clip. His hands drove the fresh clip home into the pistol as his mouth opened to scream. He spun wildly from the rope, trying to shine his light around him. He was ten feet from the surface. He shone his light over the rock walls and found the Zijin waiting for him. They hissed and shrieked and clawed at the light.

"No," he whispered, as they launched toward him. Jordan fired and in a blur of moving darkness they were upon him.

Sean and Bishop were ripped to the ground by the sudden weight on the line. The rope burned through their palms as it sped toward the hole to disappear over the edge.

Sean crawled to the hole and shone his light down into the depths. His light illuminated the dirty pond and Jordan's pack, but nothing else.

"Jordan!"

Inside the crevasse was silent and dark and still.

"Sean," Bishop whispered.

A Zijin claw arced out of the darkness and narrowly missed Sean. He rolled away from the broken planks, scrambling to get to his feet. Bishop was ready as the first one poked its head up through the floor. He fired two bullets through it.

"Jordan!" Sean shouted.

"He's gone, Sean," Bishop said. "We gotta go!"

Claws reached up through the cracked floorboards, as the reinforcements fought their way to the surface. Bishop fired as they ran.

CHAPTER 36

Sean and Bishop moved deeper into the mine through the network of tunnels, turning corner after corner. They moved steadily downward, deeper and deeper into the earth.

Up ahead was a flicker of firelight. They crept to the corner of the tunnel and peered around its edge.

Small fires had been left staggered throughout this section of tunnel, providing a weak, warm light.

The illuminated passage spiraled down and to the left. The spiral was less fortified than the rest of the mine and it occurred to Sean that they were probably near the site where the mining exploration had ground to a halt. The firelight had grown brighter as Sean and Bishop neared the end of the spiral.

At the end of the spiral they found a huge natural cave the size of an auditorium. Scattered near the mouth of the cave were the remains of mining equipment and materials. Timbers and boards cut to strengthen the tunnels lay in moldering piles, slowly disintegrating.

The two men stepped to the entranceway and peered down into the cave. Beyond a short, forty-foot rockslide of rubble, a wide flat floor fifty yards square was riddled with fires. Some raged as large as funeral pyres. Red, orange and golden tongues of flame snapped and reached for the high ceiling, hidden behind a pall of darkness and dense smoke. Others smoldered, mere embers, a breath away from extinction.

From the cave opening Sean stared in disbelief at the sheer number of Zijin.

He didn't have to count them. By the look of it, he was sure that every resident of Danaid was down there, all one hundred and seventy odd people. Men, women and children. Friends, neighbors and family. They all knelt, murmuring a chant, bent forward at the waist, their arms outstretched in a display of absolute worship toward a makeshift throne constructed of wood, carefully placed stones and pieces of metal. Only one person could command such respect.

Petra sat on the Zijin throne looking as beautiful as ever. Her eyes were bright and her skin shimmered. She looked out over her children, her family, with a small smile on her lips.

"You should go," Bishop said.

"I'm not leaving without my son."

"Your son is dead, Sean," Bishop replied angrily. "It's time you realized that. They don't play favorites. They don't take hostages. He's somewhere down there, one of them now."

"I have to know."

Bishop had nothing left to say. He stepped toward the cave entrance.

"Where are you going?"

"I came for her head, Sean."

Sean looked down into the lair and his stomach did a quick forward roll.

"You're going down there?" he asked. "You'll never get close. What then?"

Bishop opened his coat and revealed the explosives that lined the interior.

"Then at least she'll be a while digging herself out of this shit hole," Bishop replied. "Just be ready to run."

And with that, Bishop stepped into the cave.

Sean could hear him moving steadily down the rockslide. He crept closer to the edge. The hunter had reached the cave floor and moved toward the Zijin.

Sean was alone.

Boldly Bishop passed the worshipping Zijin, heading straight for Petra. His heart beat wildly in his chest. She smiled and the Zijin grew silent and still. Their black eyes followed his progress as he stepped between their ranks to their Lord and savior.

He got within ten feet of her before she spoke.

"Welcome," she said. "It's been a long time."

"Too long," he replied.

"Have you come for my surrender?"

"No," Bishop said, "I've come to kill you."

Petra cocked one eyebrow.

Sean peeked down into the cave. Again the sight of the Zijin made his head spin. Bishop moved through the rows of them, heading straight for Petra. He pulled his head out of the doorway and flattened himself against the wall to catch his breath.

"Fucking suicide," he whispered.

A grating sound brought up his weapon and his flashlight. He took a few steps back up the tunnel. The firelight threw their shadows over the walls, stretching them and twisting them as they made their way down the spiral.

"Daddy," a child's voice sang out. "Daddy."

Sean stepped farther up the spiral and saw the owners of the shadows, a tight group of five children ranging in age from five to fifteen. They crowded together in a pack, filthy, wearing next to nothing. They stared at Sean vacantly, coldly. One of them, the oldest, dragged his long black fingernails against the rock wall.

"Kevin?" Sean asked.

Sean took a step toward the group.

A small boy eased his head into Sean's light. Kevin looked thin and dirty and very pale, nearly gray.

"Why did you let them get me, Daddy?" Kevin whispered.

For the first time, Sean really looked at his son. Firelight flickered and snapped, twisting shadows over Kevin's beautiful face. Sean aimed his light at Kevin. His blue-gray eyes were black. The gray skin of his face hung from his skull in tatters, revealing the translucent skin of the Zijin beneath.

"Stay," Kevin whispered. "Stay."

Kevin charged his father, mouth open, and clamped down on Sean's shoulder, drawing blood.

Sean pried Kevin off and tossed the boy to the floor. Behind him the other children advanced. Their skin peeled, their bodies grew, bones stretching, muscles bulging. They stared at Sean with black eyes full of hate and hunger.

Sean drew his gun and aimed it at Kevin. Kevin rose, his voice no longer his own, but something deeper, ancient.

"Don't be afraid," he hissed. Kevin's lips and the fanged teeth of his mouth were stained with blood.

"Don't be afraid, Daddy."

Sean's finger curled around the trigger.

"Please forgive me." Sean pulled the trigger.

Click.

A wicked smile twisted Kevin's lips into a sneer. He opened

his mouth and with a lion's roar the entire group rushed Sean.

"You know I could have had you killed in the tunnels," Petra said. "Shredded in front of your new best friend up there, and all your little ghosts."

"What stopped you?"

She laughed. "I wanted to do it myself."

"That was stupid, but I guess you don't know where you are."

Petra rose from her throne and all the Zijin slowly rose to their knees.

"You found this place by accident, thinking it was perfect for your purpose. The mining company thought it was perfect too, back in '66. But it isn't perfect. And do you know why?"

Petra moved toward him now, slowly. Her beautiful blue eyes rolled over black. The markings of the Zijin language swirled over her skin. Her complexion dropped from ivory to the color of cement.

Bishop's hands opened and two thin tubes of explosives slid from his sleeve into his waiting palms.

"Too much fucking water," he said, and threw the explosives into the far end of the cave. The two metal cylinders rattled off rocks and finally landed near the edge of the wall.

The explosion ripped through the rock wall and floor and thousands upon thousands of gallons of water rushed into the cave.

Petra rushed him and Bishop met her halfway. They collided and Bishop's dagger pushed right through her stomach. Pieces of the cave walls and floor exploded upwards as the rushing tide shot forward, filling the cave floor in seconds. Zijin were smashed against boulders and crushed under falling rocks as the cave collapsed.

Those few that weren't killed outright were carried out of the cave on a raging current that propelled them up the path of least resistance.

Sean spun and kicked the screaming face of a small girl who was in Kevin's class. He fumbled with a fresh clip, slammed it home and fired wildly, missing his targets.

The children charged roaring after Sean. He stopped, took careful aim and fired. The little girl's face exploded in a red spray. He fired again and missed. That was all they needed. Sean fired again but they were too close. Kevin launched himself at his father and knocked him to the ground. Sean grabbed him by the neck to stop him from biting his throat, but the others kicked and punched him. Sean was fading. He couldn't hold his son. Or what his son had become. The little kid seemed to be made of iron. Sean could feel its hot breath on his face.

He heard thunder, getting closer, a roar.

Suddenly he was under water and carried away up the spiral of the tunnel. Kevin had let him go and he kicked toward the surface, gasping for air.

Bishop and Petra were locked together. His dagger kept them that way. They exploded to the surface as they passed the mouth of the cave, heading up higher and higher toward the light of day. Bishop pulled another knife from his coat and went for her throat. She dodged and batted his hand away, knocking the knife from his hand. Her hands flew at his face and throat, tearing huge gouges out of his skin.

The current slammed them from side to side against the tunnel walls, but Bishop held on. He was not losing her now.

He kicked to be above water and felt her hand on the back of his head pushing his face down. Another Zijin slammed into his back and wrapped its arms around him. And then another. The Zijin dug its nails into his flesh and anchored himself to the hunter.

Petra drifted quickly away from him. The Zijin weighed him down and he couldn't get free. He was trapped and sinking fast. Bishop twisted and kicked but it was no use. He couldn't shake the dying Zijin.

He sank into the darkness.

Sean spun through the current, slamming into walls. He kicked to stay above water, but in the dark it was all luck of the draw. He expected to smash his head on a support timber or an outcropping of rock. He braced himself for it, but it never came.

He finally did hit something. Hard. His body twisted around the thin metal bars of the spiral staircase that led up into the abandoned office buildings. He cried out and took a minute to realize where he was. He was dizzy from blood loss and the wild water ride. He could barely concentrate, let alone carry out the elaborate task of climbing a staircase. The water rose fast, splashing into his mouth, climbing over the back of his head. He thought seriously about not letting go of the staircase. The water wasn't even that cold anymore. His eyelids were heavy. His head dipped and he swallowed a mouthful of dirty water. He spit and gagged and then started climbing.

Forty feet behind him, Petra followed the curve of the mining tunnel, riding the same raging current as he, as it delivered her to freedom. She watched Sean as he neared the top of the stairs. He was struggling and weak. He shuffled through the metal door at the top and disappeared. Not far, she thought. Not in his condition. With any luck he hadn't dropped dead just beyond the door. She yearned for the chance to hurt him, maim him, and finally kill him, for what he and the hunter had done to her children. So many lives lost. Too many.

She angled her body in the dark water and directed herself to the staircase. She gripped the metal bars gracefully and hoisted herself up onto the risers. Moments later a trio of Zijin collided heavily into the stairs and scrambled up the structure after their leader.

Bishop was sinking fast. The Zijin holding him was dead. That much was clear, but he had dug his claws into Bishop, keeping him prisoner. Bishop hacked and slashed at the Zijin's hands until blood filled the water around him. Bishop was dying. He was losing his sight. His vision curled in at the edges. He skated along the rock floor of the tunnel, still carried by the vicious current, when he finally cut the dead Zijin away from him. Wraiths watched him even then. They looked to be workers. Miners, Bishop thought. Trapped in the mine forever. Never again knowing the sunlight. He wasn't about to join them. Not today.

His lungs burned from oxygen deprivation. He kicked off the tunnel floor and broke to the surface.

The water rose steadily. Only a foot of space separated the

tunnel roof and the water line. He was traveling fast. He rode the current around a bend, and then another and finally he saw it up ahead. A glint of metal. The tunnel opened up above his head and he swam as hard as he could with the current to the stairs.

※

Sean pushed through the heavy steel door and stumbled into the room where he had found Floyd Tinsel's camping gear. He sat down heavily on the unrolled sleeping bag and closed his eyes. He was awakened by the sound of grinding metal.

He opened his eyes and found Petra standing less than ten feet away. Three Zijin crawled over the walls and ceiling like huge gray insects, twisting their heads around to see him. Sean's gun snapped to the ready. He fired three times and missed. Petra smiled serenely without so much as flinching. She was beautiful, radiant. Her features softened as she drew near, her eyes almost sorrowful. A flicker of emotion that felt something like shame passed through Sean. The gun felt heavy and useless in his grip. He let it drop to the floor.

"Don't be afraid, Sean," she whispered.

It was her voice. He pushed against the wall behind him to stand. In his mind he saw her through dark water, listened to her beg him not to leave. He saw her face as he let go of her hands. He watched her pale form grow darker and darker as the Jeep quickly dropped out of sight.

"No, you're gone," he whispered.

"I am not gone, Sean," she replied. "I am here for you. For always."

And she smiled a beautiful smile that warmed Sean through his wet clothes. It was a welcome balm to his many wounds, beyond logic and practical thought.

"We're all here for you," she said, her voice smooth and soothing, and very near. He didn't see or hear her move closer to him. It was as if she glided. He could almost feel her breath on his face. "Me, and Kevin. Forever."

His body shuddered under her fingertip. She was inches away now. The markings swirled restlessly over her pale skin. Her breath was sweet, her skin cold, like the dead touch of frozen metal. And something else pulsed beneath her skin, something alive and wanting, a vibration, a hum of some great engine cycling faster and faster. He could see it behind her eyes. Petra was gone. All that remained was a thin, beautiful shell.

Sean moved away from her touch, from her coldness. He watched her through the frozen distance between them, watched the woman he had loved disappear in front of him. The symbols stopped swirling and lay flat and stagnant, darkening her skin to a dull gray. Her voice sounded like the voice of an angry crowd, a warrior nation. She did not scream. She barely spoke above a whisper. Her eyes glittered with contempt.

"You will be beautiful."

Sean spat in her face.

"Fuck you."

Her right hand opened, no longer a hand. Her long, black fingernails hooked into a talon. She stabbed Sean just below the ribcage, digging her nails through his flesh, punching through his stomach. Blood filled his mouth as he tried to scream. She lifted him off his feet and tossed him toward the far wall where he crumpled in a heap against the floor. The waiting Zijin swarmed him like a pack of hungry dogs.

Bishop burst through the metal door and in one smooth motion shot and killed all three Zijin. Petra charged him and he fired into her chest four times. She was blown backward in a red spray of blood and slammed against the far wall.

Bishop squatted in front of her, grabbed a fistful of her hair and drew his dagger. His blade cut through the air aimed just below her porcelain jaw. Petra grabbed his wrist out of the air and twisted it viciously, breaking it. Her right hand fired up under Bishop's jaw and launched him backward through the air.

"You should have stayed dead, hunter."

Bishop was on all fours when she delivered a powerful kick to his face that sent him reeling backwards. He rose again, slowly, and on all fours. He stared up at her and smiled, his mouth dripping blood onto the tile floor.

"You're dead," he whispered.

Petra stomped the top of his head, driving his face into the ground. He made no sound. He rolled onto his back where he lay helpless, his arms at right angles to his body, palms up, waiting.

Sean lay in a heap against the wall, not moving. The metal staircase creaked just beyond the steel door. More Zijin had found their way up from the depths. Soon they would be here. Sean rolled to his side and saw a pistol lying on the floor about five feet away. Bishop's gun.

He could hear the Zijin on the stairs. There was no time. He could barely see, let alone move. Every muscle and tendon in his body screamed. He had to keep blinking to keep his eyes from closing. His breathing was getting harder and harder, as if he were breathing through a flattened straw. He left a wide blood smear on the floor as he crawled toward the pistol and scooped it up off the ground.

Bishop closed his eyes again and felt the bones in his face knit together, felt the ragged tears in his skin reach for each other across each wound. He slipped to his hands and knees and Petra kicked him onto his back then dropped heavily onto his chest, straddling him. Petra's eyes were black. Her pale skin was alive with the swirling symbols of the blood figure. Her smiling mouth opened to reveal three rows of razor-sharp teeth. She pulled Bishop's head up by his hair, and exposed his throat. Blood fell from Bishop's lips as his eyes threatened to slip closed.

"You are nothing. Your reign is over," she said, "We will rip through your streets. Your children. Your families. Everything will be ours. We are the next step. The next *leap* in your evolution."

Bishop's eyes rolled open and he stared into her face, flushed and shaking with rage.

"You're history," he whispered.

Three quick gunshots erupted. Petra's chest exploded outward in a gush of red where three bullets ripped through her. Petra dropped Bishop's head and turned to Sean. The smoking gun trembled in his bloodstained hand. Petra's snarl curled into a smile as she laughed until her shoulders trembled. Sean watched helplessly as her wounds stopped bleeding, and quickly narrowed to pinpricks as her body healed itself.

"Fool," she hissed. "Pathetic."

Bishop looked to his right where his dagger lay. He stretched his fingers and they landed on the edge of the hilt. He edged it closer with his fingertips until he could grip the handle.

Zijin thundered up the spiral staircase. They flooded through the metal door and poured into the open space, shrieking and chittering.

Petra was still laughing as she turned back to Bishop. Before the smile disappeared from her lips, a second mouth opened across her throat. Petra fell backwards, clawing at her sliced windpipe as blood poured from the wound.

Sean screamed and threw the gun at the charging horde but they raced forward. They fell upon him, biting and clawing. Sean cried out and flailed his arms but there were too many of them. His screams were smothered by the writhing mass.

Bishop dragged himself across Petra, straddling her as she writhed beneath him, squirming and gurgling, her black eyes wide and terrified.

Bishop held his blade in his right hand. She raked her nails over his arms, reaching for his face. Her jaw snapped as her body bucked beneath him. She spat blood as her legs thrashed.

The Zijin reached out for him, their powerful bodies charging hard. "Goodbye, Eve," Bishop whispered, and with one swift motion he sliced her head from her shoulders.

Brilliant white light exploded from her squirming body.

The blinding white light filled the room, incinerating the charging Zijin where they stood. The light poured through the hallways like a sudden flood, blasting away shadows, blowing

open doors and breaking what windows remained in a brilliant
white flash.

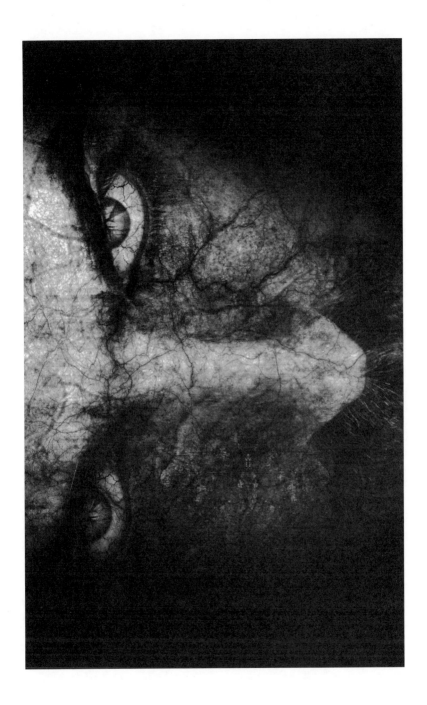

EPILOGUE

During the following week, a short-lived epidemic swept through eight different countries and put health organizations around the globe on full alert as thousands of otherwise healthy citizens died, seemingly from natural causes. No one could understand it. No infection was ever detected, no dreaded virus, no poison. Religious groups began calling it the Rapture or Armageddon, depending on which camp you belonged to. Almost all the faiths believed it was a sign from God. Or the Devil. Again, it all depended on which camp you put your lawn chair in.

The victims varied in age from eight to eighty-two. They were schoolteachers, doctors, pizza delivery boys, elementary school students. They were your friends and neighbors. Normal, everyday people. Or so it seemed to the general public.

The Ministry of the Wraith knew otherwise.

The screams began six months later.

They led Bishop Kane back to Danaid.

Once again he found himself walking through the familiar rows of tombstones. Of course now the graves were all but obscured by the long grass and thick weeds that had sprung up since the previous winter. No one had taken over the cemetery since Norman and the rest of the town of Danaid had disappeared. No one dared. No one even visited the town now that the FBI and state police had left. It had quickly become a modern day ghost story and web sites popped up everywhere to speculate about what really happened. The theories ranged from alien abduction to a massive cult suicide. Bishop figured it wouldn't be long before the thrill seekers and ghost chasers would come to the small Alaskan town. They would tear up pieces of floor or steal anything with a splash of blood on it to sell on eBay to other sick freaks who reveled in that sort of thing. But not yet. For now he was alone.

He pushed farther north through the weeds and a light rain that fell from a slate colored sky. The crowd of wraiths waited high on the hill. Among them, Norman Conklin looked on silently.

Bishop carried the shovel over his shoulder as his feet whispered through the long grass between the plots. The gnarled trees, now full with leaves, rustled softly in the growing wind.

As they neared the grave, the cries grew louder. Finally, he arrived atop a gentle rise. Three plots were spaced close together, mother and father on either side of their young boy. The grave of the young boy remained empty, as his body had never been found.

The sky had darkened since Bishop had left the driveway of Norman's old house, and now looked miserable. Black and blue, it threatened to drop more than a sprinkle of rain as thunder rolled close to the earth.

Bishop drove the shovel into the sod and pried up a healthy chunk

His breath rose in banks of fog. He worked relentlessly, his arms swinging in rhythm, clearing the dirt like a machine. The muffled cries that rose from the grave grew louder with every shovelful of dirt that Bishop removed.

Finally, the blade of Bishop's shovel struck wood. After a few more loads, he was on his knees, sweeping the dirt away from the coffin lid, finding the seam with his fingertips. The man inside scratched at the lid, calling for help, his fists pounding at the ceiling of his prison. Bishop cleared the rest of the lid and instantly, hands from within forced the lid open.

The man's eyes were wild and jacked wide as he pushed past Bishop and scrambled up the wall of the grave onto the wet grass. His suit coat, split up the back, flapped in the wild wind.

"Sean Berlin," a voice whispered from the dark.

The man spun to meet its owner as a woman clothed in a hooded black cloak suddenly stood very near. She moved without sound. With delicate hands the color of bone, she raised the hood of her cloak high enough to allow Sean to see her eyes, like chips of jade.

"Sean Berlin," the woman repeated, her voice as smooth and as light as smoke. "You will see a world beneath the one you know, a layer of life hidden from most. I can offer this only once."

Bishop leaned against a nearby tombstone and watched Sean as he weighed Madeline's offer. Sean tilted his head to the boiling black sky and the rain beat a rhythm into the smooth white skin of his face. Then Sean returned his gaze to Madeline, his mouth carved into a smile.

"Welcome to the family," she whispered.

About Patrick McNulty

Patrick McNulty's dark fantasy *Sleepers Awake*
is based on his screenplay *Dark Season*.

A lifelong fan of horror and fantasy fiction, this is his first novel.
Patrick McNulty is a Medical Technician in the Canadian Armed
Forces. He is working to complete a degree in Neuroscience.

He lives, when not on assignment with the military,
in Petawawa, Ontario with his wife and two children.

KÜNATI

Kunati Book Titles

•••••••••••••••••••••••••••••••••

Provocative. Bold. Controversial.

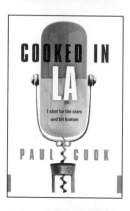

Cooked in LA ■ Paul Cook

How does a successful young man from a "good" home hit bottom and risk losing it all? *Cooked In La* shows how a popular, middle-class young man with a bright future in radio and television is nearly destroyed by a voracious appetite for drugs and alcohol.

Non Fiction/Self-Help & Recovery | US$ 24.95
Pages 304 | Cloth 5.5" x 8.5"
ISBN 978-1-60164-193-9

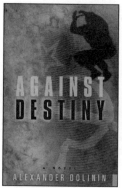

Against Destiny
■ Alexander Dolinin

A story of courage and determination in the face of the impossible. The dilemma of the unjustly condemned: Die in slavery or die fighting for your freedom.

Fiction | US$ 24.95
Pages 448 | Cloth 5.5" x 8.5"
ISBN 978-1-60164-173-1

Let the Shadows Fall Behind You
■ Kathy-Diane Leveille

The disappearance of her lover turns a young woman's world upside down and leads to shocking revelations of her past. This enigmatic novel is about connections and relationships, memory and reality.

Fiction | US$ 22.95
Pages 288 | Cloth 5.5" x 8.5"
ISBN 978-1-60164-167-0

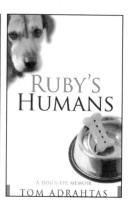

Ruby's Humans
■ Tom Adrahtas

No other book tells a story of abuse, neglect, escape, recovery and love with such humor and poignancy, in the uniquely perceptive words of a dog. Anyone who's ever loved a dog will love Ruby's sassy take on human foibles and manners.

Non Fiction | US$ 19.95
Pages 192 | Cloth 5.5" x 8.5"
ISBN 978-1-60164-188-5

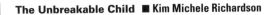

The Unbreakable Child ■ Kim Michele Richardson

Starved, beaten and abused for nearly a decade, orphan Kimmi learned that evil can wear a nun's habit. A story not just of a survivor but of a rare spirit who simply would not be broken.

Non Fiction/True Crime I US$ 24.95
Pages 256 I Cloth 5.5" x 8.5"
ISBN 978-1-60164-163-2

Save the Whales Please
■ Konrad Karl Gatien & Sreescanda

Japanese threats and backroom deals cause the slaughter of more whales than ever. The first lady risks everything—her life, her position, her marriage—to save the whales.

Fiction I US$ 24.95
Pages 432 I Cloth 5.5" x 8.5"
ISBN 978-1-60164-165-6

Screenshot
■ John Darrin

Could you resist the lure of evil that lurks in the anonymous power of the Internet? Every week, a mad entrepreneur presents an execution, the live, real-time murder of someone who probably deserves it. *Screenshot:* a techno-thriller with a provocative premise.

Fiction I US$ 24.95
Pages 416 I Cloth 5.5" x 8.5"
ISBN 978-1-60164-168-7

Touchstone Tarot ■ Kat Black

Internationally renowned tarot designer Kat Black, whose *Golden Tarot* remains one of the most popular and critically acclaimed tarot decks on the market, has created this unique new deck. In *Touchstone Tarot*, Kat Black uses Baroque masterpieces as the basis for her sumptuous and sensual collaged portraits. Intuitive and easy to read, this deck is for readers at every level of experience. This deluxe set, with gold gilt edges and sturdy hinged box includes a straightforward companion book with card explanations and sample readings.

**Non Fiction/New Age | US$ 32.95 | Tarot box set with 200-page booklet | Cards and booklet 3.5" x 5"
ISBN 978-1-60164-190-8**

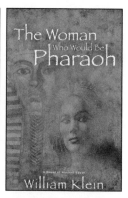

Sleepers Awake
■ Patrick McNulty

Monstrous creatures invade our world in this dark fantasy in which death is but a door to another room of one's life.

**Fiction | US$ 22.95
Pages 320 | Cloth 5.5" x 8.5"
ISBN 978-1-60164-166-3**

The Nation's Highest Honor
■ James Gaitis

Like Kosinski's classic *Being There, The Nation's Highest Honor* demonstrates the dangerous truth that incompetence is no obstacle to making a profound difference in the world.

**Fiction | US$ 22.95
Pages 256 | Cloth 5.5" x 8.5"
ISBN 978-1-60164-172-4**

The Woman Who Would Be Pharaoh
■ William Klein

Shadowy figures from Egypt's fabulous past glow with color and authenticity. Tragic love story weaves a rich tapestry of history, mystery, regicide and incest.

**Fiction/Historic | US$ 24.95
Pages 304 | Cloth 5.5" x 8.5"
ISBN 978-1-60164-189-2**

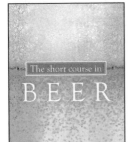

The Short Course in Beer
■ Lynn Hoffman

A book for the legions of people who are discovering that beer is a delicious, highly affordable drink that's available in an almost infinite variety. Hoffman presents a portrait of beer as fascinating as it is broad, from ancient times to the present.

Non Fiction/Food/Beverages | US$ 24.95
Pages 224 | Cloth 5.5" x 8.5"
ISBN 978-1-60164-191-5

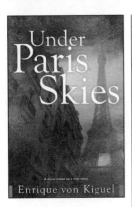

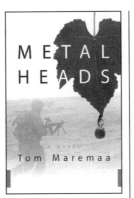

Under Paris Skies
■ Enrique von Kiguel

A unique portrait of the glamorous life of well-to-do Parisians and aristocratic expatriates in the fifties. Behind the elegant facades and gracious manners lie dark, deadly secrets

Fiction | US$ 24.95
Pages 320 | Cloth 5.5" x 8.5"
ISBN 978-1-60164-171-7

Metal Heads
■ Tom Maremaa

A controversial novel about wounded Iraq war vets and their "*Clockwork Orange*" experiences in a California hospital.

Fiction | US$ 22.95
Pages 256 | Cloth 5.5" x 8.5"
ISBN 978-1-60164-170-0

Lead Babies
■ Joanna Cerazy &
Sandra Cottingham

Lead-related Autism, ADHD, lowered IQ and behavior disorders are epidemic. *Lead Babies* gives detailed information to help readers leadproof their homes and protect their children from the beginning of pregnancy through rearing.

**Non Fiction/ Health/Fitness &
Beauty | US$ 24.95**
Pages 208 | Cloth 5.5" x 8.5"
ISBN 978-1-60164-192-2